Secrets
by Necessity

by

Jane Drager

This is a work of fiction. Names, characters, places, and incidents are either the product of the author's imagination or are used fictitiously, and any resemblance to actual persons living or dead, business establishments, events, or locales, is entirely coincidental.

Secrets by Necessity

COPYRIGHT © 2013 by Jane Drager

Cover Art by *Debbie Taylor*

The Wild Rose Press, Inc.
PO Box 708
Adams Basin, NY 14410-0708
Visit us at www.thewildrosepress.com

Publishing History
First Champagne Rose Edition, 2013
Print ISBN 978-1-61217-708-3
Digital ISBN 978-1-61217-709-0

Published in the United States of America

Charles put one boot up onto the porch and leaned against a post. They stood at eye level. They also stood too close. The magnet pulled her again. She had this overpowering urge to lean over and kiss him. She wanted to feel his arms around her; she wanted to taste his lips. She wanted to feel his strength, his power.

She wanted her breath back. Alex clutched the blanket closer to her chest instead.

She had no right to want this man. It was merely a physical attraction, nothing more, a hormonal urge to be satisfied. She told herself over and over he wasn't interested. Common sense said not to get involved. Alexandra Colter was a visitor with no plans to stay. She belonged in New York. She had enormous bills to pay. She had neither the time nor energy to get involved with anyone, especially a man so far away from her home base.

Dedication

To Mom,
who supported me in my many endeavors.

Chapter One

Alexandra Colter stepped out of her car with trepidation. The cabin stood before her, a ramshackle dump that was to be her living quarters for the next seven days. Her best friend recommended this little getaway. Billings Mountain, Virginia. Quiet, remote—the perfect place to relax. A step back in time to escape the noise and pollution of New York City. Even the realtor who arranged the reservation said Rosebay Cabin was the nicest of the bunch.

They both had to be on drugs.

The cabin looked weather-beaten and neglected, a forgotten relic lost among the trees. Its construction consisted entirely of logs with a roof covering an open, beat-up porch. A hammock swung lazily on one side while large wooden slat chairs sat close to a heavy wooden door. In contrast to the cabin, the hammock and chairs came right off a store shelf.

Cedar shingles covered the roof, most with curled edges and broken pieces, giving every indication that buckets caught the rainwater on the floor inside. *Spiders and woodworms and mold spores, oh my*!

"I must have 'sap' stenciled on my forehead," she grumbled.

Good money, down a rat hole. Literally. Money she scrounged up and saved. Money she couldn't afford to toss into the wind. How was she supposed to relax

1

when every creature known to man would be crawling on her skin? All she wanted was a quiet place to sit with her feet up and do nothing. A whole week of nothing. The realtor never said to bring a can of bug spray.

Alex sighed heavily and stepped away from the car. While she stood contemplating whether to approach the place, a big hunk of man walked around the side of the cabin carrying an armload of wood. His sheer physical presence stunned her. Chest and arm muscles bulged through a light cotton shirt while strong legs carried him and the wood with ease. A football player without the padding. She stopped breathing. All the apprehension she felt coming here, alone and so far from her home base, dissipated at the sight of the strength he displayed. She stared with unblinking wonder, and she would bet money that her heart jumped into A-fib. She braced herself to meet a new and different world, but nothing like him.

His steps faltered when he saw her. Two eyes like black marbles showed surprise. "Can I help you?"

A baritone. Nice. Sensual and stimulating. Perfectly suited for the body. She shook herself. "Are you Charles?"

"Yes."

"I'm Alexandra Colter. I was told you'd be here."

A black eyebrow twitched, but his face changed into a stoic stone. What brief friendliness showed with his words disappeared with a flash. It was not an encouraging sign.

"You were told I was coming, right?"

"I'm expecting a man, Alex Colter, M.D."

"Well, that's me."

He eyed her carefully with eyes direct and

2

unwavering. "You don't look like a doctor."

"Hopefully, I don't look like a man either."

He shook himself. Part of that stoic stone went with it. "I'm sorry. I didn't mean that the way it sounded. Welcome to Rosebay Cabin, doctor. Follow me inside. This wood is heavy."

Eight logs in one arm. He carried them as if they had the weight of a straw. Handsome and strong. An attractive combination. *Might turn into a decent vacation after all*...if she could get beyond this hellhole of a cabin. She let him lead the way inside just to see if the porch supported his weight.

It did.

The man was a lumberjack in the true sense of the word with broad chest and shoulders packed into a six foot two frame. He had a dark and formidable presence, like a hovering storm cloud threatening to release its load. He moved with the grace of a man comfortable in his own skin, a man used to hard work, rugged and confident and giving every impression of fighting off a pack of wolves with one hand and a yawn. She actually felt a hormonal surge just staring at his broad back.

She followed him in.

At the sight of the interior, Alexandra unabashedly gasped. Outside, the cabin showed ill-use and age, neglected beyond help. Inside, back to the 21st century. Modern kitchen to the right, king size bed to the left, and a potbellied stove dead center surrounded by a cushioned sofa and two matching chairs. She stopped in her tracks.

Charles stacked his wood by the stove and turned. "Surprised?"

"Very. I almost put the car in reverse when I saw

the place."

He nodded knowingly. "Happens every time. All the cabins are like this. Done on purpose to create an illusion of living like our ancestors who lived and worked on these mountains. No television but there is a stereo, a complete kitchen except for dishwasher, and of course, a modern bath—over here."

The bathroom was off the side of the bed. Thankfully, the toilet wasn't a hole in the ground.

"This is the smallest of the cabins," he continued. "We built it for a honeymoon couple or a person like you who wants a quiet place alone. What do you think?"

"The place is one very big room," she commented still staring in awe. She looked up at the vaulted roof. No light seeping through. No buckets on the floor either. "I like it."

"Everyone is surprised when they see the transition. You'll notice several places on this mountain that look untouched by time."

"The gas station for one. Definitely 1950's. I especially liked those mechanical pumps."

He studied her. "You stopped for gas?"

"Yes. My car sucked on fumes halfway up. I met Harry, the gas station owner. Nice guy. He showed me how the pumps worked."

A pair of black brows crunched together in a frown. "He should have called." He took out his cell phone. "Someone usually notifies me if they see one of our guests arriving...ah, my fault this time. My volume was too low." A pair of full lips pursed as he read a text message. Such a serious man. Hardly any expression emanated from his eyes. They usually made good poker players.

"Your forewarning came too late, Charles. I'm already here."

"Indeed." He reread the message, looked at her, then reread it again. "You impressed Harry."

"I only got gas."

Analytical eyes studied her. He clearly debated. Then, a decision made, he showed her the message. *Guest arriving. Rosebay. Melting time.*

She looked up at him after reading it, puzzled. "That doesn't sound like I impressed him. What do you have to melt?"

Both eyebrows shot upward as he stared. Forget the poker face. The man was clearly surprised. Alexandra cringed. "I missed something again."

His face finally relaxed. No smile came to his lips yet, but at least some of the storm cloud lifted. "Harry is referring to your looks," he said.

"Oh." She blushed.

Dammit! Alex silently cursed her parents for leaving out that one gene which would help her see when a man expressed interest. They did a good job of creating a petite brown-haired, brown-eyed beauty with flawless skin and straight white teeth, but to this day, she needed friends to point out what usually flew over her head. And why did she have to blush so damn easy? It made her look like a naïve schoolgirl. She hated that friggin' gene, too.

She caught his amused gaze. "I don't often hear something so bold from a stranger. New Yorkers tend to be a bit, er…aloof."

"I didn't mean to embarrass you," he said, "but I am surprised to see how easily you blushed. It's refreshing to discover a woman who isn't full of herself. A rare quality these days." He put his phone away. "Will anyone be joining you?"

She walked over to the sofa and brushed her hand across the soft fabric. "No, I'm it, Charles." Then as an afterthought, she turned and said, "Is that okay?"

"More like unusual for a woman. Why?"

That startled her. "Why, what?"

"No woman should ever be alone these days. It isn't safe."

She shrugged. "I'm used to it. You don't grow up in the slums of Newark, New Jersey, without learning how to survive on your own. Besides, it isn't unusual for a woman to be alone in New York." She probably shouldn't have told him something so personal. It revealed a vulnerability too early in the game here. She hardly knew the man. He could be a mass murderer who tortured poor, lonely women for the hell of it.

Not like she was lonely. She grew up alone. She lived her life alone, a fact accepted at an early age. She wouldn't know how to live differently.

"There's no room service," he continued. "Our cabin cleaner is once a week on Saturday. You won't see her tomorrow since she cleaned the place today. The linen closet in the bathroom is stocked with fresh towels. Don't hesitate to use them more than once to save on water. Used towels go in the hamper." He walked toward the kitchen. "You are responsible for cleaning up any mess in the kitchen. The cabinets are stocked with whatever utensils you need. If you need something special, just ask. Filters for the coffee maker are in the cabinet above." He opened the cabinet and showed her. "All food supplies are your responsibility."

He closed the cabinet and faced her. "Any questions?"

"No, sir." The man barked out instructions like a drill sergeant. She nearly saluted.

"I'm available twenty-four hours a day. My cell number is on the refrigerator door along with fire and police." He tapped the white sheet taped to the door to draw her eyes to it. "Don't hesitate to call if you have a problem. I take care of all seven cabins on this mountain. I'll stop at the occupied ones at least once a day, which right now is every one. You won't even know I'm here. Let me show you a few things outside."

The midget in the shadow of the giant. Her whole life was the midget in the shadow of a giant. With a height a whisper above five foot one, she looked up at everyone. Men, women, even some children. She lacked "tall" genes as well.

Maybe she was adopted and no one told her.

Charles led her to the back of the cabin toward a square metal box. Beside it stood a large woodpile. "This is the electric generator," he said while tapping the lid. "You will always hear the hum of the motor. You see where the woodpile is. This way, miss—I assume it's miss." He stopped to face her. "Either someone isn't paying attention, or it's your choice."

Her head jerked up. "What are you talking about?"

"Most New Yorkers who come here tend to be a bit standoffish. I don't see that in you at all."

"I still don't get your point." If he had one. They just met and already the man puzzled her. "If you're asking why I'm still single, I think that's too personal a question."

"I find being direct saves time."

Like he gave a shit whether she was married or not.

Oh.

A chuckle reverberated from deep within her throat. "My friends call me a space cadet. I miss everything."

"Like Harry's message."

More than Harry's message. A wink, a flirt. She never caught the heads that turned when she walked through the hospital wards. Patients, visitors, staff. Oblivious to all. Some men came right out and asked her to sleep with them. She was so damn dense otherwise.

Like now.

They walked a short distance uphill to a lone wooden bench. It sat ten feet from the cliff edge and faced a magnificent view of the lower valley and beyond. The view drew her like a magnet.

"Wow!" she said with a gasp. She had never seen anything so magnificent.

"Perfect place for a bench, wouldn't you agree? The city in the distance is Roanoke. It's about 150 miles from here sprawling out in all directions. It's a long ride considering we have no direct route. In air miles, it's about 85."

"I can watch a sunset." She said it stupidly with eyes glued to the distant mountain range. "I've never seen one."

He looked at her as if she just stepped off an alien spacecraft. "You need to get out of the city more, doctor."

Out of the damn hospital would be more like it. Sunrise, sunset, she saw neither, too many tall buildings in the way, too many years surrounded by steel and stone, too many hours cutting and stitching up wounds.

She should have a Vitamin D deficiency.

"You must be tired after your long ride," he said suddenly. "I won't keep you much longer. Come this way."

He led her back to the cabin and toward the forest opposite. She looked everywhere with the eyes of a city girl. The forest thick with trees. Large boulders without graffiti. Shrubs and weeds with tiny flowers. A squirrel forayed for buried nuts. A chipmunk already found his. Both cheeks bulged as evidence. So cute.

Charles stopped. Alex collided right into his back. It felt like a brick wall with no give whatsoever. "Sorry," she mumbled.

A strange expression crossed his face. It disappeared as quickly as it appeared. He turned and pointed to a stone path that cut through the forest.

"This path leads to Henrietta's general store," he said. "She is also our postmaster. The walk is three quarters of a mile one-way on fairly level ground. Most people take advantage of the path. Let me help unload your car."

She popped the hatchback, but he only stopped to stare. "You drove all the way up the mountain in this?"

She looked at her bright orange Yugo with more dinks and dents than a scrap yard reject. "I came all the way from New York in that," she corrected.

He stood back, incredulous. "A doctor wouldn't drive a car like that!"

"A doctor with no money would." She looked at it proudly. "Best investment I ever made. Bought and paid for by me. It got me here."

"It's a tin can!"

"Don't insult my vehicle. You'll hurt its feelings."

Alexandra grabbed her medical bag and purse.

Charles shook himself then grabbed everything else.

"You didn't bring much," he stated as they entered the cabin.

"It's only for a week."

"Most women pack like they're moving in. There is a flashlight in the kitchen drawer. You'll need it after sunset if you venture outside. Please be careful. It gets dark out here. I don't want you to fall off the cliff. Is that everything from the car?"

Suitcase by the bed, bag of foodstuff on the kitchen table, bag of reading material by the sofa, backpack and hiking boots by the door. "Yes, that's everything."

"Not much food either although you don't look like you overindulge."

"I really didn't know what to bring. I couldn't take perishables on such a long ride."

He nodded in agreement. "Henrietta stocks just about everything at the store. Don't hesitate to take a walk. Here's your key."

The key dangled from a leather strap with the name "Rosebay" burned into the hide. Quaint. He turned to leave but stopped by the door. He stared down at the backpack. "By the way, miss, be careful when you're out hiking. I see you've never done it before."

Her eyebrows shot up. "How would you know?"

He pointed downward with a slight degree of impatience showing on his face. "The price tags are still on the backpack and boots."

"Oh." She snickered. "No, I never hiked before. The extent of my athletic prowess is a jog around Central Park every Sunday after rounds." Any more than that and she would burn off what little fat remained on her body. That meant no boobs. Bad enough she weighed all of a hundred pounds.

"Keep my cell number handy when you're hiking," he recommended. "I know this mountain better than anyone. I'll be the first to find you if you get lost. I suggest you take the backpack with you when you go to Henrietta's. It's better to stuff that than to carry a bunch of bags. Anything else I can do for you before I leave?"

Like jump in the sack? Dear Lord! She never had such a thought hit her so quickly. "No, thanks, Charles. You've done enough."

"I'll keep you supplied with firewood, but you saw where the wood pile is if you need more. There's no central heating in the cabins. The stove is designed to keep the place sufficiently warm. Nights get chilly up here. Matches are in the kitchen drawer. Remember, if you decide to stay more than a week, let me know." He turned to leave.

"Charles."

He stopped in the open doorway. "Yes, miss?"

She hesitated. "Do I tip you?"

He cocked an eyebrow. "You can if you want. You can also wait until you leave. This isn't a resort where people wait on you hand and foot, but I'll do things for you if you ask...within reason. From the sound of it, you don't get out much."

She shook her head. "Too busy being a doctor."

The stone face returned. She wondered why the statement wiped the relaxed one away.

"A commendable profession," he said through tight lips, "but it should not be your life."

Funny that he said the very words that forced her to

11

take a hard look at herself. She had no life outside the hospital walls. It took an overwhelming schedule for that realization to sink in. She went home to an empty apartment. She ate alone; she slept alone. After one exhausting shift, the loneliness hit like a brick.

And it shouldn't have. She spent her entire life alone because of two hard-working parents working two jobs apiece. She depended on no one out of necessity. She learned to be strong and determined at an early age, and those traits traveled with her straight through to medical school and beyond. That was why she thought nothing of booking a week of solitude at a quiet mountain cabin.

Old habits die hard.

She should also have her head examined.

She realized with a start that Charles was gone. She heard no vehicle start up and drive away, no heavy boots on the porch, not even the sound of the door closing. In a blink, he was gone.

One other point struck Alex as she stood in the middle of the cabin floor. Silence surrounded her, an eerie, mind-boggling silence. She heard only the faint hum of the generator behind the cabin. Nothing else. No overhead planes, no impatient car horns, no skateboards rolling on concrete. Zip. She felt stone deaf.

She liked it.

Chapter Two

Alexandra had difficulty putting a diagnosis to her emotions after Charles left. New feelings certainly. An exuberance perhaps, a "finally on vacation" exuberance. Definitely not sadness. She loved her job and enjoyed every aspect of it, but it consumed her time and thoughts. Burnout was inevitable, and she was too young for that. Hell, she hadn't paid off her student loan yet. A vacation was essential, a luxury denied for too long. She purposely chose Billings Mountain to remove herself far from her world of medicine. Unfortunately, she placed herself in totally unfamiliar territory, alone, isolated, surrounded by forests instead of brick. It felt odd.

She sighed heavily and checked her watch. A sunset should perk up her mood. She hurried out to the bench half-afraid the sun would set without her. As before, that fabulous view drew her. An awesome sight. Picture-perfect in every way. A thick woolly green blanket complete with clumps of nap covered the entire valley. It spread itself over the surrounding hills to keep everything warm and cozy. An unobstructed sunset waited as it slowly descended behind the western mountain range. Alex sat on the bench to watch. Her first ever.

A rustling to the right startled her. Scared the shit out of her actually. Her head snapped in the direction of the sound, her senses alerted. Charles gave a lot of information before he left, but he never mentioned about wildlife on the mountain. Deer, yes, to be expected, but what else? Wolves? Grizzlies? Mountain lions? And God forbid, snakes?

A second rustling. Alexandra put her feet up on the bench and hugged her knees while staring intently in the direction of the sound. A few seconds later, the setting sun glowed on a blond head of hair. That surprised her. "You can come out. I won't bite."

The blonde head retracted into the brush along with something red in color. The patter of running feet followed and quickly faded into the forest. A child without question. Probably checking out the new guest at Rosebay.

Alex let out a long sigh of relief and turned her attention back to the sunset. It poked along, milking the moment, slowly inching downward until it disappeared behind the ridge.

End of show. Much too short. Lights clicked on down in the valley and beyond. A lovely sight. Peaceful. Quiet. A world settling in for the day. And turning incredibly dark. She stood reluctantly to her feet and strolled back to the cabin.

She slept soundly. She put herself right in the center of that king size bed and felt like a queen. She expected the awesome quiet to keep her awake, but she hit the bed and went out. She woke fully refreshed and ready to start a new day.

While sipping a cup of tea, Alex stood near the potbellied stove with a look of scorn on her face. She tried to start it last night without success, and the cabin lost whatever heat it held. She contemplated turning on the oven. She often did that when the furnace went out in her apartment building. Then she would run to the hospital to get warm. She needed to learn how to build a fire quickly or spend the rest of the week wearing extra clothes.

She threw on her jacket and took her cup of tea out to the bench by the cliff.

A gentle fall breeze blew the steam rising from her teacup. It blew the scent of pine with it from the forest. Alex sucked in a large breath to push out some of the New York soot coating her lungs. It felt so good she did it again.

She immediately went into a coughing fit. Obviously, her lungs were not used to fresh air.

A twig snapped somewhere below the cliff edge. A second snap increased her curiosity. She stood to peer over the ledge.

Far below, young trees jutted out of deep crevices along a straight cliff wall. It resembled a large nest where a bird could lay her eggs and still have room for a sofa. To the left, the mountain sloped downward at a more leisurely angle with a forest of trees thick and forbidden. A hawk circled, searching for prey. Buzzards, too, waiting for leftovers.

"You're up early."

Alex whirled, spilling half her tea in the process. "Shit, Charles, you scared me!"

"Sorry. Didn't mean to especially with you standing so close to the ledge. Weren't planning to jump, were you?"

Her eyes scanned the big man standing on the other side of the bench. He looked fresh from a shower, his black hair slicked back and damp. His face was closely shaven and scented with a pleasant after-shave that filled the morning air. A very masculine specimen. Big, brawny, and beautiful. Hardly any comparison to the men she worked with in New York.

She wanted to just stare and drool. She shook herself instead. "That was a strange thing to say. Of course, I'm not going to jump."

"My mistake. We've never had a woman stay here alone. Men, yes, but never a woman. I worried about you all night. I guess I'll worry about you tonight as well."

"How many men jumped off the cliff?"

One eyebrow shot up. "None."

"So what makes you think I will?"

"You're alone. It must be for a reason. Tell me I'm wrong."

"That is hardly a valid argument. You are very wrong. Just because I'm a woman alone doesn't mean you should be drilling me on my purpose."

"You can't possibly like it."

The little badger in her sprang to life. That same little badger always fought tooth and nail with her medical superiors for a patient who couldn't afford healthcare. Charles practically threw down the gauntlet by challenging her lifestyle, and the badger never refused a challenge. "I not only like being alone, I insist on it. Am I making this statement clear enough, Charles?"

He studied her long and hard with unreadable eyes. They told her nothing, not even friendliness. The man obviously made a practice of hiding his emotions.

"Clear enough," he said. "I apologize for the intrusion. I stopped by to see if everything was satisfactory."

"Yes, everything is fine except for the heart attack you gave me. You shouldn't sneak up on people. If you had a vehicle, I'd hear you coming."

"I'm too cheap to buy gas." He half-sat on the back of the bench by lifting one leg. "I drive a beat-up red pickup truck. Not much better than yours in fact. You'll know it when you see it, but at this time of year, the weather is perfect. I enjoy being on foot. I'll try to make some noise the next time I stop by."

Another snap brought her attention back to the cliff. A black bear and two cubs meandered through the trees and rocks on the slope about a hundred yards down. The crunch-crunch of the underbrush beneath their feet echoed upward as if they were only two feet away. She watched with fascination as the mother lumbered, searching for food while the cubs played with—

Alex started. *The cubs played with a head*?

She stared, hoping the distance played tricks with her eyes. She could be mistaken. No, she was not mistaken. She didn't get her medical degree from a cereal box. Where the hell did they dig up a head?

"Charles, look at this." She waited for him to come alongside. She pointed to the cubs. "That's a head they're rolling around."

He peered down the cliff. "That's a rock."

"Rocks don't have hair. Take a closer look."

He continued to peer down the cliff. A deep frown formed. "It could be a head. It's possible they got into the cemetery again. I'll check it out." He stepped away from the ledge and faced her. He looked huge with the backdrop of the landscape behind him. For some reason, she put the bench between them.

"Did you sleep well?" he asked.

"Like a rock."

"Good. I hope you enjoy your stay with us. Good morning, miss."

He left as quietly as he came. He disappeared into the forest before she had a chance to blink.

Alexandra returned to the cliff edge to peer over the side. The bears were gone, the head with them. She knew anatomy, and even at this distance, she recognized a human head. If she was wrong, she would eat her teacup.

She returned to the cabin.

Time for a hike to the general store. Alex grabbed her wallet and cabin key and stuffed them in her jacket pocket. She debated taking her cell phone. The debate was short-lived. She hadn't turned it on since she left New York. She wasn't about to turn it on now. Good news or bad, she wanted none of it. She threw it back into her purse.

With hiking boots on, the empty backpack draped over one shoulder and all price tags removed, she set off down the stone path.

A slight mist hovered close to the forest floor. She swung a foot through it just to see it separate and come back together. She did this several times; a type of battle of wills maneuver, Alexandra Colter against the mist. It won every time.

A tunnel came into view. Right in the middle of the forest! An artwork of intertwining tree limbs and branches stretching for several hundred yards above the path. In her mind, she entered an enchanted forest with visions of leprechauns and silver white unicorns. She heard the singing flowers caroling as she walked and watched little fairies zipping from bush to bush. Her imagination ran wild. Like any little girl left alone too long, she read fairy tales and dreamt of Prince Charming saving her from the slums. Common sense prevailed even as a child. She knew Prince Charming was a myth. The happily-ever-after crap was for the privileged few, never to touch the little girl who felt like Cinderella sitting in her own little corner. She learned early to cope with the dismal loneliness of never having anyone around.

Even now. But something was different about this Billings Mountain. She couldn't put her finger on it. She was alone here, yes, but not alone, if that made any sense. Charles, for one. The little blonde, for another.

She'd figure it out.

The path led to a wooden bridge. She peered over the rail to watch a stream of clear water flow by. No fish that she could see. Some kind of a bug skimmed along the surface. Nothing else. She moved on.

The path eventually widened, the forest opened up, and before long, Alex stood on the asphalt parking lot for Henrietta's General Store. Two vehicles sat in parking slots. One was a red pickup truck that had seen better days. Charles' no doubt. No exaggeration about the condition either. The poor thing had half its paint peeling and rust holes by the wheel wells big enough to put a baseball through. And he had the nerve to comment on the condition of her Yugo.

The second vehicle was a black Camaro. Alex wondered whether it belonged to Henrietta when a woman hurried out of the store carrying a canvas shopping bag. She stood tall and sleek with flaming red hair draped over her shoulders. She stopped short at the sight of Alex on the asphalt. No smile spread on her lips, but she stared through dark Prada sunglasses, her face rigid. Alexandra gave a little wave only to be polite, but she knew it was a crapshoot. The redhead got in the black Camaro and sped off, squealing her tires all the way.

"And a good morning to you, too," Alex said as the car disappeared around a bend. She opened the screen door and stepped into the building.

Henrietta's General Store came straight out of a western movie. Wood everywhere, wooden beams, wooden floor, wooden shelves. To the left along the wall stretched a long wooden counter broken into two sections. At one end, an old mechanical cash register sat perched and ready to use. To the right was the post office partitioned off from the rest of the store by a door and gated teller's window. It was behind the teller's window where an older woman glanced up. She did a subtle double-take with a look of surprise passing across her face. She smiled politely. "Be with you in a minute."

"No hurry."

"Honey, we don't hurry up here on Billings Mountain."

Alexandra already figured out that piece of news from the moment she drove onto the mountain and watched Harry stroll toward her car. She wandered around the store.

Shelf after shelf stretched the length of the store. There was a section for hardware, a section for aches and pains, then canned goods and dry goods, breads, homemade desserts, and munchies. Lots of munchies.

High up on the walls hung old signs of various shapes and sizes, tacked and arranged in a first come, first hung kind of way. The place was homey, woodsy, and definitely low tech.

"Now, how can I help you?"

Alexandra turned to see the woman from the teller's window directly behind her. She was a tall woman, perhaps five ten, of sturdy build, in her late sixties with long salt and pepper hair tied in a bun. She wore blue jeans with a blue cotton vest over a thick sweater. The vest had a Welcome to Billings Mountain logo embroidered on the right upper corner. She had inquisitive brown eyes, full lips, and creamy chocolate skin that was absolutely flawless. If her beauty failed to cause a stir, then her sultry voice did it for her.

"Are you Henrietta?"

"Yes, Henrietta Carlson. You must be Dr. Colter, our Rosebay guest. Pleased to meet you." They shook hands. "Charles told me to expect you. He said you didn't take much food."

"I'm afraid I'm not carrying a lot of cash."

"You don't need cash. I can make an imprint of your credit card, and I'll add all your purchases to it. When you're ready to leave Billings Mountain, I will send the bill in. How's that sound?"

"It sounds perfect."

Henrietta walked behind the counter. "We try to make it as hassle-free as possible for our guests. Put your backpack on the counter and grab a basket. We stock just about everything. If you don't see it, ask. It may not be out on the shelf yet since the truck just came in."

"Speaking of truck, is that Charles' truck out

there?"

"If it looks like it belongs in a scrap yard, yes. He calls it the Red Baron. The thing is a piece of crap. However, the man loves it, and a new one is out of the question." She fussed with a piece of hair that fell from the bun. "He usually parks it out front at this time of year. He's quick to tell you that he can get to places faster on foot because he knows so many shortcuts. He grew up on this mountain so he should know."

At that precise moment, the screen door flew open with a bang. A little girl ran in, tears streaming down a pair of dirt-smudged cheeks.

Alexandra's blonde peeper from yesterday.

Chapter Three

The little girl had dirt smudged all over her clothes, face, and hands. Wet mud covered both knees of her blue jeans and the little boots on her feet. In her left arm, she clutched an equally dirty red Elmo doll while she held the other arm out in front of her, hand extended. She ran straight for Henrietta.

"My goodness, Lucy, what's wrong?"

She held up a finger for Henrietta's inspection. Tears streaked the dirt on her cheeks but not a sound rose from her throat.

"A splinter," Henrietta said after inspection. "Don't worry, little one. I'll get it."

Henrietta reached behind the counter and pulled out a tattered cigar box. She dumped the supplies onto the counter: alcohol, gauze, tweezers, pin needles, Band-aids. A homemade splinter removal kit. She lifted Lucy onto the counter with a grunt and a groan, but just then, the phone rang in the post office cubbyhole. Henrietta's face changed to one of exasperation, and she glanced quickly at Alex.

"Do you want me to get the phone?" Alex asked.

"No, it's probably the call I've been waiting for. Would you mind taking care of Lucy?"

"Why, of course, if she'll let me."

Henrietta hurried to answer the phone. Alexandra faced Lucy who eyed her warily, sniffing. "Now, let me see what we have here." She said it lightly, hoping to alleviate the little girl's fears.

Lucy offered no resistance when Alex took her hand. She was without doubt a very striking little girl. She could not be more than five years old with straight golden hair and a pair of extraordinarily big blue eyes emphasized by long golden lashes. She sat sniffing while round eyes followed Alexandra's every move.

"You're my little friend from yesterday," Alex said as she cleaned Lucy's finger. "You didn't have to hide, you know. I won't bite. My name is Alex."

Most children say "Alex is a boy's name", but Lucy remained silent, still sniffing, her eyes intent on her finger.

"Hopefully, Elmo didn't get a splinter, but I see he's all wet. Did you drop him in the stream?"

She nodded vigorously.

"You jumped in to save him and probably got the splinter from the bridge."

Lucy stared in awe.

"I'm sure Elmo appreciates your saving him. He was lucky you were there." Alex put a Band-aid on her finger. "All done except for one thing." She kissed the little finger before lowering Lucy to the floor. Lucy held up Elmo. "You want me to check him?"

Alex squatted to Lucy's eye level and took Elmo from her hands. She put on her professional face while examining him. Very serious. She turned him this way and that, scrutinizing every seam. "Aside from being wet and dirty, I'd say Elmo came out of his ordeal just fine. He should give you a big hug for saving him." She handed the doll back.

Lucy immediately clutched Elmo to her chest. In

one quick move, she reached over and kissed Alex on the cheek before running from the store.

Henrietta stood directly behind Alex as she straightened up. Her brown eyes were intense, analytical.

"She's a lovely child," Alex said, slightly startled at the intensity.

"Yes, she is." Henrietta grabbed a tissue and handed it to Alex. "You handled her well."

"It was only a splinter." Alex took the tissue but looked at Henrietta in question. Henrietta pointed to Alex's left cheek. The tissue came back dirty.

"A splinter to us is nothing. To a child, a tree limb. What kind of doctor are you?" She took the tissue and tossed it in the trash.

"Surgeon."

"Then that splinter was right up your alley. I'm impressed."

Big deal. Stitching an arm back on would be impressive. "Lucy seems shy."

"We can't tell. She hasn't spoken a word in over a year."

Alex stared with surprise. "Why?"

"We don't know. She's had every conceivable test, but they found nothing wrong."

"What about intelligence?"

"Normal for her age. She displays normal curiosity, too, but she will not speak. She has been silent since the accident. It upsets me to even talk about it."

"Then don't talk about it. It's none of my business."

The door opened. Charles walked in, looking big and imposing. He filled the entire doorframe with his bulk. He stopped short when he saw them, debated noticeably whether to continue, then a decision made, walked directly to the coffee maker sitting at the far end of the counter.

A strong hormonal surge shot through her as he passed. The man was without doubt unlike any she ever met. His presence demanded attention whether he asked for it or not.

"She just met Lucy," Henrietta told him. "I think it's a good idea to tell her about the accident."

"She doesn't need to know." He said it firmly. Curtly would be a more descriptive word. His very tone defied debate.

"It's none of my business," Alex insisted.

"Nonsense," Henrietta said, unperturbed. "Lucy never kissed a stranger before. You made a new friend, doctor."

"It's none of her business," Charles repeated even more firmly.

Henrietta glared at him. Charles only stared into his steaming coffee cup without making eye contact with either of them.

Alexandra distinctly felt the tug of war. On one side, Henrietta, openly willing to talk. On the other, Charles, tight as a clam. This duel piqued her curiosity, and she wondered why such a difference of opinions.

"I could say something really clever right now," Henrietta growled in that deep sultry voice, "but I won't since we have a guest standing here." She turned to Alex. "Don't mind him, dear. He's being hard-headed and stubborn."

"I usually sedate them."

Henrietta started. Then she laughed. "Hammer or

pill?"

"Needle. Much faster."

Henrietta roared with laughter. "I'd say we humor him because he can't stand needles."

Charles shifted uncomfortably. "I wish you two would stop talking like I'm not here."

"You can't take down a bull with a hammer," Alex said.

Henrietta roared even harder. Her brown eyes sparkled. "I like you, Dr. Colter."

"Call me Alex." Then to Henrietta's puzzled expression, "Short for Alexandra."

"Oh, no, dear, you are much too beautiful for a name like Alex. I will call you Alexandra."

The phone rang in the cubbyhole again. Henrietta looked toward the area with a sigh. "I'm still waiting for that phone call." She hurried toward it.

Charles watched Alex over his steaming coffee. The clam refused to open, she thought. Was he always like this or was it just because she stood before him? Either way, there was no sense pushing the subject. She grabbed her basket.

"Where are you going?" he asked.

"Shopping. I need some stuff."

"Don't you want to hear about the accident?"

"I don't want to come between two friends. It's obvious the two of you share different views." She found herself in the cookie aisle. So much to choose from. She grabbed a few packs.

"Well, get back here and let me tell you before I change my mind. Want a cup of coffee? I'll buy."

Alexandra strolled back and put her basket up on the counter. "I could use a cup." More than a cup actually. Tea never cut it for her in the morning, but she had no cream. In her mind, coffee without cream was punishable by death. Charles poured and handed a cup to her. In that brief exchange, their hands touched. An electric jolt shot straight up her arm. It surprised her, and she met his gaze. He had a bemused expression guarded by half-veiled eyes. She quickly looked away and loaded her cup with cream.

He stared at her cup as if it boiled right before his eyes. "Why don't you have a little coffee with your cream?"

"I like it this way. You, I see, drink it black. Ugh!" Then, in defiance, she poured more cream into her cup. "I thought you said this accident was none of my business. Why the change of mind?"

He studied her over his steaming cup. "Did Lucy really kiss you?"

"Yeah, it's no big deal."

"Yes, it is a big deal, doctor. She has shown affection only toward Henrietta. She's afraid to approach the rest of us. You just met her."

"Lots of patients kiss me. It's my natural charm." Henrietta's sultry voice chuckled from within the cubbyhole. Charles found no humor in it. "Maybe Lucy is starting to break out of her shell."

"Maybe." He said it thoughtfully, still studying her.

"Are you going to tell me about the accident or should I sit down and put my feet up?"

Charles made a face that looked to be a combination of reluctance and annoyance. Finally, he took a deep breath and sighed. "Tom and Cindy were Lucy's parents. All three were in the car when it went over the cliff, just about two miles up the mountain.

Tom and Cindy were killed outright. We found Lucy dangling from her car seat. Her neck and shoulder were broken. It was a miracle she wasn't paralyzed." He sipped his coffee, watching for her reaction. She gave no reaction. Nothing surprised her anymore.

"Lucy spent months in the hospital," he continued. "She hasn't made a sound since. No laughs. No cries. Nothing. She had no other family so Henrietta took her in. She felt Lucy belonged with us on this mountain."

"Yes, and I'm afraid I can't put her in school next year because she just won't speak." Henrietta rejoined them. "The girl is not stupid. I read to her almost every night. I know she reads along with me, but she won't say the words out loud."

"The trauma of the accident is obviously keeping her locked up," Alex suggested.

"No kidding." Charles said it sarcastically prompting another glare out of Henrietta.

"She may need more time," Alex said, undaunted. "Are there other children to play with?"

"Yes, but she doesn't seem interested," Henrietta said. "She spends most of her time alone with Elmo."

"You can't suggest anything we haven't tried," Charles said angrily. "Doctors think they can butt into everyone's life—"

"*Charles*!"

Their eyes locked. Fire flew out of Charles' eyes as he glared at Henrietta. She responded with her own hot glare. What the hell was going on between these two?

Alex touched Henrietta's arm. "I'll handle this, Henrietta." She faced Charles with as much defiance as facing one of her professors. "For your information, big boy, I enjoy what I do. I'm good at it, and most people are grateful. I'm not in it for fame or fortune, but I am in it to help people. I don't know who said what to you about doctors, and frankly, I don't give a damn, but don't take it out on me. I'm a guest on this mountain, and I expect you to treat me accordingly."

She learned early in her career how to handle obstinate patients. In their eyes, she was either too young, too pretty, or too small. They soon found out that Dr. Alexandra Colter was the best surgeon her side of Manhattan, and she let them know it. Only Charles wasn't a patient. His anger at her was different, more deep-seated and personal. She wondered why.

"What caused the accident?" *Pushing buttons, Alexandra.*

His face changed to stone. She kept herself nonchalant by sipping her coffee.

"We don't know," he said through tight teeth. "Tom was a good driver, and the investigators couldn't find anything wrong with the car."

"Except it went over the cliff and no one knows why," Henrietta finished.

"Suicide?"

Wrong word. Charles' face turned to ice. She immediately felt the chill. She decided to end the conversation before his friendship with Henrietta suffered irreparable damage. "I better get my shopping done." She put her cup down and grabbed her basket.

None of my business. She repeated the phrase over and over. *None of my business. Lucy is not my patient, this mountain is not my hospital. I am a stranger with no right to butt in.* She always managed to put her foot up somebody's ass. More than once, it got stuck.

The screen door slammed. The truck started with a

roar and sped away. She never looked up. Finished with her mental shopping list, she took her basket to Henrietta who now stood behind the counter.

"I'll apologize for him because I know he won't," she said sadly.

"His anger will consume him."

"Very perceptive of you. He's convinced that if we had a doctor on the mountain, Tom and Cindy would have survived. He's wrong, of course. They were dead before we reached them. Finding Lucy alive was bittersweet." She shook herself then forced a smile. "Is this it?"

"One last thing." Alex ran to get cream from the refrigerator. Quart size. "That's it." She handed Henrietta a credit card. Henrietta took a modern calculator out from under the counter and punched in numbers. "I thought you used this old thing." She pointed to the mechanical register.

"I do when the sale is simple, and a child is watching." Her fingers moved swiftly over the keypads. No arthritis in that hand.

"Why don't you have a doctor up here?"

"We can't get one interested enough to stay. Lord knows Mr. Billings has tried. That's H.C. Billings, the owner of this mountain."

Alex's brows shot upward. "A man owns this mountain?"

"Yes, so even he would like to see a doctor on it. Our nearest clinic is 70 miles away. A long ride when you don't feel too terrific."

"Then Charles is expressing the anger of everyone on the mountain."

"I wouldn't put it that way, dear. He is angry with

the wrong people for the wrong reason. Doctors visit, stay in one of our cabins—like yourself, then they leave. Each time he gets more bitter because it is eating him up inside. It's not like we're isolated. We have a helipad at the elementary school for our severe emergencies. Our ambulance squad handles everything else."

"You just don't have a doctor in residence."

"Correct."

"Because of that, he will be angry at every doctor who pays a visit."

"Correct again. Don't get me wrong, Alexandra. Charles is usually a reasonable man. Just a little misguided." She glanced up. "Maybe you can help him."

"*Me*! The man wanted to wring my neck. Forgive me, Henrietta, but I'm not a psychiatrist. Most of my patients are unconscious and lying on a table."

"I'm sorry. I shouldn't have brought it up. You're a guest here, and I apologize." She ran the credit card through the reader. "All done. Here's your card." She packed the groceries into the backpack. "Now you can come in and tell me what you're taking out. We will finalize the bill before you leave. If there is anything special you want, let me know. We aim to please here on Billings Mountain."

"I should be fine. I'm only here for a week."

"Then I hope your stay with us is a pleasant one. It's very nice to meet you, Alexandra. If you get lonely up at the cabin, don't hesitate to pop in for a cup of coffee. I always have a pot brewing. And don't worry about Charles. I doubt you'll see him much. For the most part, he keeps to himself and hardly bothers with our guests. He can be quite charming when the mood hits him."

"I doubt I'll see any of that charm." She grabbed the backpack and draped it over one shoulder. "If he can't be civil with me, then I'd appreciate it if he stayed out of my sight."

"I'll relay the message."

Alexandra wasn't sure why she said it or why she even gave a damn. She was on vacation, dammit!

Chapter Four

A surprise waited when Alex returned to the cabin. Heat hit her as soon as she opened the door. Wonderful heat. It flowed out of the potbellied stove as if it had a fan hidden behind the logs. She knew who started it even without asking. She confirmed her suspicion when she turned toward the kitchen. A second surprise waited. A small vase full of colorful wildflowers stood centered on the table. A note sat under it.

Dr. Colter:

I see you tried to get a fire started. You put in too much wood. This makes it difficult for the fire to breathe. I started it for you. Add a log now and then to keep it going. You won't need much heat for a cabin this size so don't overdo it.

The flowers are native to this mountain. If I had known you were a woman, they would have been on this table when you arrived.

Charles

Henrietta was right. The man could be charming. Alex debated whether this charm emerged before or after his gaze cut her in two. She wanted to think after as a form of apology. Common sense told her before. He left the store too angry to gather flowers then start a fire without causing the whole place to burn down. Logic had its advantages.

Definitely before.

She put away her groceries.

Since such a gorgeous day beckoned, she decided to sit out and relax with one of her medical journals. She flipped through her pile, found the one she tried to read twice already, and stepped outside.

The hammock gave an enticing little sway. She debated. The bench with its fabulous view? She'd never read there. She'd sit and daydream instead. The chairs with its wooden slats? Her ass would hurt after a time. The hammock with its gentle sway? Absolutely. It looked too comfortable to pass up. She settled in and opened her journal.

****

A noise registered in her sleepy brain. She let it pass until the unmistakable presence of a watchful pair of eyes alerted her senses. She woke with a start to see Charles leaning against a post. The anger of earlier was gone, but his gaze held an intensity that threw her completely off guard. She jerked, forgot about her mobile bed, whirled and hit the porch with a thud. He never moved.

"Have a nice nap?" he asked.

"You scared the shit out of me! Again, dammit!"

"Sorry. I didn't want to wake you. You looked very comfortable."

"I was—with the emphasis on *was.*" She rubbed her bruised elbow. "What time is it?"

"A little after 4:30."

Four thirty? She yawned. "I slept half the day away. I never would have done this back home." Never would have had the time either. She shook the sleep out of her eyes.

"That's what Billings Mountain is all about, doctor.

It's a place to relax. You can sleep all day if you want. Very peaceful. I stopped by to see if you needed anything."

Henrietta said he never bothered with the guests. He himself said she would hardly know he was around. Yet, here he stood for the second time today. Was he doing his job or was it something else? She looked at him suspiciously.

"How many times a day do you pop in on your tenants?" She immediately regretted the words. His eyes turned into slits.

"You don't need anything." He said it harshly and spun on his heel.

"Wait a minute! Aren't you going to help me up?"

He turned back. "Why, did you break something?"

"A gentleman always helps a lady to her feet."

"You look the independent sort to me." He retraced his steps.

She made a face at him and stood to her feet—without his help. "Chivalry is dead," she said sadly.

"No, it isn't. Just the medieval definition of it." His face relaxed. An amused curl to his lip came with it. He put one boot up on the porch. "My job is not to kiss your ass, just make sure it's comfortable."

"Fair enough. I was afraid your animosity toward me would ruin my time here."

His whole face twisted with surprise. "Animosity? That's hardly a word to use."

"It describes my perception. It certainly isn't southern charm you're throwing at me."

She dusted off her clothes, fully aware that his gaze followed every move. She should feel uncomfortable being alone with a man so powerfully built, especially a man she hardly knew. He stood close enough to reach and overpower her, but for some reason, she trusted him. She hadn't a clue why.

Just a feeling.

"Tell me what your perception is," he said softly.

She glanced at him. "No."

"I'd really like to know."

"No, you wouldn't."

"From you, yes, I would."

She doubted the sincerity of the statement. Nothing changed since the general store. He had a chance to cool down of course, but she was still an object of scorn. She debated while studying him. "What word would you use to describe how you treated me at the general store, Charles?"

He stepped back, shocked.

"Yeah, see! Animosity. You're angry. It can't be because I'm a woman who is independent—your own words—nor is it from anything I've done since I haven't been here long enough. So, it must be because I'm a doctor who wasn't around to save your friends."

Oh, God, if looks could kill. A bright shade of red rose from his shirt collar while his lips pressed together in a thin white line. The anger boiled out of his eyes, more so than at the general store. She expected him to explode in a fit of rage. Instead, he turned on his heel without another word and took off down the drive.

Oops! Overstepped her boundaries. Again. Even on vacation, she couldn't stop this friggin' habit of helping people. Why should she even care what he thought of her profession? Hell, half the patients in the hospital complained about all doctors being quacks. She picked up her journal and entered the cabin.

A nice shot of caffeine would perk her up right about now. It should help her forget about this man who *usually never bothered with the guests*. The same man who *kept to himself*, who hated doctors, who started her stove and decorated her table with flowers. The same man who stopped by twice already. So many contradictions. She needed strong coffee to drown her confusion. And cookies. Coffee and cookies. *Yes, perfect.* She put the coffeemaker together. While it dripped, she took out a bag of cookies and two mugs.

Just a hunch.

The knock sounded on the door before the coffee finished brewing. It took a lot for him to come back, she knew. The man had pride, no doubt about it. "Come in, Charles."

He stepped in and stood looking at her. His gaze was direct and unwavering. The anger disappeared from his face, but unfortunately, she couldn't comprehend what replaced it.

"I made coffee," she said in case his sense of smell was shot to hell. She invited him to sit at the table.

He stood rigid and unmoving. He watched her for the longest time with eyes that slowly let the hurt show. Finally, he took one step away from the open door.

"People rarely challenge me," he said.

She shrugged. "My profession forces me to be a little more up front with people. It gets results. You can close the door."

He closed the door and then walked toward the table. The man with the formidable presence. The cabin was way too small for him. And something else. She got a sense of a man hurting far more than he let on. Why that particular flash of wisdom came to mind puzzled her. She had a hard enough time understanding men without suddenly being so astute.

"Are you a man pretending to be strong for everyone's sake, Charles?"

He jerked. "I don't know what you mean."

She wasn't sure what she meant either. "You look like you might break down and cry."

His dark brows came together in a scowl. "Men don't cry."

No, they just bottle it up and have heart attacks and die. Maybe she was wrong. "My mistake."

"I'm the one who should apologize," he said. "I took my anger out on a stranger, a stranger who happens to be a guest on this mountain. It was inappropriate and wrong."

"Black?" she asked with coffee pot in hand. He nodded. She, of course, loaded her cup with cream. "Not all deaths are explainable," she continued. "I can tell you that based on experience. Doctors are not the miracle workers people want us to be. You need to let it go. Be thankful Lucy survived. She is a lovely little girl." Alex sat at the table.

Charles did not sit. He did take the offered cup of coffee. She pointed to the bag of cookies, but he declined. "How'd you know I'd come back?"

"No clue." It wasn't a lie. She really had no clue. Her only thought was a kinship because neither one of them had enough money to buy a decent vehicle. She bit into her cookie. Chocolate chip. Her favorite. Charles obviously had a change of mind and reached into the bag. He took a cookie and popped the whole thing in his mouth.

"These will spoil your dinner," he said.

"This *is* my dinner. I'm on vacation, remember?"

One eyebrow cocked. "I'm guessing you can't cook."

"You guessed right. I make no pretense about it."

"Let me guess again. A privileged childhood."

Alex stifled a laugh. "Far from it. The poorest of the poor."

His face grew suspicious. "Most doctors I know led pampered lives."

"Well, knowing how you feel about doctors, I'd say your opinion is biased. I know quite a few like myself who struggled to meet tuition. In fact, I have yet to pay off my student loan."

The loan was the one thing tying her to an exhausting surgery schedule. Once she paid it off, she could actually get a life, maybe move out of New York and work in a small community hospital. *Yeah, dream on.*

"How old are you?" he asked.

"That has nothing to do with a basket of beans."

He started. "I think the expression is 'can of beans.'"

"Whatever." She took another cookie. "You're not supposed to ask a woman's age."

"You look too young to be a doctor."

She smiled up at him. "Thank you. I hope you can say that when I'm 80. You, of course, are older than me."

His eyes narrowed. "How would you know?"

"I'm a doctor. I know these things. You have a fabulous physique for a guy approaching 40." She realized too late what she said. She stared into her coffee cup to hide a rising blush. A fruitless maneuver.

He put his face close to hers.

"I'm 34," he said. "A far cry from 40." He pulled back after grabbing another cookie.

"I'm 31." This man should not be affecting her so quickly. A lot of good-looking men approached with bold propositions. She never blushed in front of them. What made Charles so different with just a simple look? Granted, she felt an attraction that was hard to shake, but really now. She wasn't a sexually starved do-gooder. "The cookies might spoil your dinner, too."

"Nothing spoils my dinner."

She looked at him. "Please don't tell me you cook like a French chef."

"Not even close. You'll get the basics from me."

He watched her over his coffee cup. She watched him right back. It was a comfortable silence. He was in no hurry to leave, and she was in no hurry to get rid of him. She liked the way his gaze roamed over her. She followed suit by roaming all over him. Something warm touched her gut when their eyes met. She blamed it on the coffee. "Any luck with the head?"

He started. "Head? Oh, right, I checked the cemetery. Nothing disturbed. James and I will search the cliff side when he gets back from the valley."

"Who's James?"

"Our police officer. I told him what we saw." He popped another cookie. "I doubt it will amount to anything. A doll's head maybe."

"Awful big doll's head," she mumbled. An adult head without question. "Thanks for starting my stove." A safe subject. Better than talking about body parts.

"You're welcome. I should have realized a woman from New York wouldn't have a clue about starting one."

"That is a sexist remark, Charles, even if it is true. And thanks for the flowers."

"Flowers are routine whenever a woman stays in one of our cabins. We started the tradition years ago."

She fingered the flowers. "Well, it's very thoughtful. I needed a bit of cheering up."

"So I suspected. I saw sadness in your brown eyes yesterday. That's why I was up half the night worrying. I thought you came to do away with yourself."

"Toss myself off the cliff, you mean?" She shuddered. "Pills would be easier." She sighed heavily. "Stress nearly did me in. I'm struggling to pay off a loan, and every doctor in the hospital knows I won't refuse to cover a shift or be on-call just to make extra money. It leaves me with little time to breathe. This vacation was essential because I'm a little too young for burnout." She sniffed the flowers. An unusual scent. Woodsy. Sweet and woodsy. "I still have to go back and start all over again though. It's not a fun thought."

He sipped his coffee while watching her. Then, he completely relaxed. His eyes brightened while his body gave a heavy sigh and dropped its shield. A human stood before her. The man with the formidable presence evaporated. She liked what she saw.

"I hated college," he said. "In fact, you're looking at a man who got thrown out of Yale. Yes, Yale. Close your mouth, Doc." He sat opposite her at the table. "My father was furious. He was an old Yale man and thought I should follow in his footsteps. An authoritarian in every sense of the word. He bullied my mother, and he bullied me. He thought I threw my entire future away. I even got married hoping to calm him down. It didn't work. We got divorced two years later." He sipped his coffee. "Thankfully, no children were involved, but it was a nasty divorce nonetheless. I became the caretaker after that. I'm better with a hammer than I am with a pen. Even my father admitted to that."

She refilled his cup whether he wanted it or not. He looked relaxed and at ease. Yes, she thought, the drill sergeant was at ease.

"My father was a difficult man," he continued. "He tried to control every aspect of my life. It became even worse after my mother died. To the people on this mountain, he was the nicest man alive. To his one and only son, he was my commanding officer. I was expected to jump whenever he spoke."

"Makes sense," she mumbled.

"What?"

She jerked. She realized too late she said the words out loud. "You have a drill sergeant way about you, Charles. That's a son emulating his father. You're the man in charge now."

He sat back, surprised. "Yes, I am like my father. Maybe I need someone to remind me when I'm barking out orders." He frowned, deep in thought. "It comes with the territory."

That made absolutely no sense. "Care to elaborate?"

"No, at least not yet."

Part of the shield rose. She wondered if he revealed too much to her. Not like she could make heads or tails of it. "Why didn't you move away?"

He shook his head. "I love this mountain. I grew up here." He swallowed the last of his coffee and stood to his feet.

"Did I really look sad yesterday?" She didn't feel sad. Tired maybe, but not sad.

He peered at her for the longest time. Then slowly, warmth flowed into those coal black eyes. She almost thought he would smile, but no, that was clearly an illusion on her part.

"You have expressive eyes, doctor. Even now. Your patients must fall in love the second they meet you. If you don't believe me, then you need to look in a mirror more often." He stared at the floor, his eyes unseeing, his face thoughtful. Then his gaze shifted to meet hers. "You know, you could find a less stressful job. Why don't you come down here with us?"

"It's not that easy."

"Sure it is. Just pack up and wave bye-bye. Think about it. Folks around here will love it. They'll finally have a doctor on the mountain." He eyed her carefully. "You'll never be alone anymore."

"I like being alone."

"Oh, cut the crap! My guess is you're in denial. No one likes to be alone all the time."

"I like my life the way it is, thank you." She glared up at him. "I'm reminding the drill sergeant to cool it."

He grunted. "I'm stating a fact, and you know it." He placed his callused hands on the table and leaned over, forcing his face into her space. "Promise you'll keep an open mind."

She pulled back, startled. "Why?"

"Are you one who breaks a promise?"

"No," she said, puzzled.

"Then promise."

"We sound like two little kids, Charles." She sat

back, totally amazed.

"Promise me." He grabbed her forearm, not gently either. The move surprised her. Even more surprising was the stimulation it caused. Her entire gut flipped.

"All right, all right, I promise to keep an open mind. Just don't tell me you're gay." She almost laughed at the expression he shot back at her. He released her arm and straightened up.

"Do you really think I'm gay?" he asked, incredulous.

"I'm praying you're not." *Oh, God*! She blurted the words without thinking. She stared into her cup.

He again leaned across the table and put his face close. She had the unmistakable urge to kiss his lips just to feel if they were as soft as they looked. His lip curled mischievously. "I'd screw you in a second if you let me," he growled.

A challenge? No one challenged Alexandra Colter and got away with it. Their eyes locked. "Careful what you wish for, big boy."

He shot back, surprise written all over his face. She almost laughed. "I'm not an angel, Charles. I enjoy a good round of sex once in a while."

His face changed to a scowl. "Animals have sex."

"Yeah, but humans enjoy it more." She quickly got up from the table and grabbed the two mugs, hoping to hide the rising blush. She couldn't believe she said what she did. To a stranger even! His growl, his touch, his eyes caused indescribable sensations, new sensations that were as foreign as this mountain. She didn't understand them one damn bit. She clunked the mugs into the sink and resisted the urge to splash cold water on her face.

"I also want a promise that you won't leave without telling me," he said with authority.

She gratefully allowed the change of subject. "Yes, I'll promise that, too." The commander spoke. She thought male doctors were bossy as hell, but this guy beat them by several yards. "You may as well call me Alex."

"Well, I'm Charles, not Chuck, not Charlie, just Charles." He extended his hand. She took it, aware that his one hand equaled three of her own. The pact was sealed.

"I'm thoroughly confused," she said, "but you have my word. What brought this on?"

He ran a hand through his dark hair without the slightest care that several strands stood on end. "Call it a necessity. The women I meet these days disappear without so much as a goodbye. I'm beginning to develop a deep psychological complex. I'll leave you now." He turned toward the door.

"One more question, Charles." She followed. "I'd like to try hiking tomorrow. Any particular direction I should take?"

"Any direction will do. Be aware of where the main road is, and you will always find your way back. Don't try to cover the mountain in one day. There's a lot to explore. Pick up a walking stick as you go. You can use it in case an animal approaches. And carry your cell phone with my number on speed dial. Take something to eat and drink and have a good time." He turned to leave. Before he reached for the doorknob, he snapped his fingers and turned back. "Can I have your cell number? This way, I'll know immediately who it is."

She gave it to him. "I haven't turned my phone on since I left New York," she admitted.

"But you *will* carry it with you tomorrow, right?"

"Yes, sir. I will take it with me."

Overly bossy or protective? She decided protective. It felt nice—and somewhat unusual. She spent her entire life alone, first as a latchkey child and now as an adult. No one really gave a damn where she went. His simple request pulled her in faster than she cared to admit. "I really don't mind how many times a day you stop by, Charles."

He cocked a surprised eyebrow but said nothing in answer. With a wave, he was gone.

She couldn't for the life of her figure out why she said that.

Chapter Five

Alexandra took Charles' advice and put his number on speed dial. To do so, she needed to turn on the phone and damned if there weren't a bunch of voicemails waiting. She listened to none of them.

Some other time.

She hadn't slept like a rock last night. For the first time in her life, a man clouded her mind, a man who forced her to question her lifestyle. She liked being alone...didn't she? She tossed and turned all night because of that one stupid question. Of course she liked being alone. She grew up that way. She was used to it, and it never bothered her. So, why did the question roll around in her head all night?

Charles, of course. He brought it up, damn him. He should try growing up in an inner city instead of this gorgeous mountain full of forests. Being alone became a safe haven of sorts, a chance to keep away from the violence on the streets. When she moved to New York, the pattern continued. No regrets either.

Alex was just tying on her boots when the roar of a vehicle vibrated the windows. She recognized the deep sound of a big engine and confirmed it with a quick glance out the window. The Red Baron came up the drive with a huge cloud of dust behind it. She stepped onto the porch as Charles pulled up.

"I was hoping to catch you before your hike," he

said as he stepped out.

"Well, you did. What's up?"

"I need a big favor, and it's not a pleasant one." He approached the porch. "We found the head—and the body. We need a medical examiner."

Her eyes went wide as she stepped back in shock. "I don't have that kind of experience, Charles! You need a forensic specialist, not a surgeon."

"We need a doctor, Alex. James is the forensic expert. He has the background and can handle all the details, but he needs a doctor before he can move the body. It's not a pretty sight, and I'm not forcing you into it. If you refuse, I'll understand."

Dear Lord, she never expected something like this. She hardly knew what to say. "Do you know who it is?"

"Not yet. It's badly decomposed, and James won't move the body until you get there to see if any ID is under it. Will you help us out?"

She hesitated. This was new and a definite departure from surgery. Still. *Yuck*!

"I don't want to ruin your vacation," he said, "but you'll save us an awful lot of time. If you refuse, we'll wait for the county medical examiner. He's out on a homicide so it should only take five, six, seven hours tops before he gets here."

She should refuse. She'd hated her rotation in the morgue during med school. The smells were indescribable, not to mention the formaldehyde gave her a headache for a week.

"I won't push you," he said softly.

The anxious look in his eyes weakened her though. She sighed heavily. "All right, I'll give it a try, but I make no promises."

"Great. I'll drive you over."

They headed downhill on the main road until reaching what looked to be a service road hidden amongst trees. The Red Baron proved a capable vehicle, bouncing over ruts and crevices without complaining. Before long, they entered a small clearing where a Billings Mountain police cruiser sat. A man in a police uniform leaned against the cruiser, waiting. He looked up as the Red Baron approached then stepped toward them.

Alexandra's breath caught. The man was the most gorgeous creature this side of heaven. He had golden blond hair and blue eyes that nearly did her in. She sat there mesmerized until Charles threw open her door.

"Alexandra Colter, meet James Thomas," Charles said with some restraint.

She damn near melted when they shook hands. The man was without question movie star quality. She thought it best to get down to business. "Where's the body?"

"Down there." James pointed to the cliff.

She stepped back, shocked. "You guys expect me to go down there?"

"You'll be all right," Charles said. "I'll lower you and James simultaneously. He'll instruct you as you go. It's a slope, Alex. Just try to stay on your feet."

"And don't look down," James said. "Look at me and follow what I do."

Looking at him won't be a problem. But mountain climbing? "I must be out of my mind," she mumbled.

Charles fitted her in a harness, put a helmet on her head and gave her a pair of leather gloves. She felt like a little girl being dressed by her father except this man had an unfathomable affect on her. All sexual. He kept his face serious, but their eyes met more than once, both locking, both hesitating, both looking quickly away. James was similarly suited plus he wore a large backpack. Charles positioned the Red Baron closer to the cliff edge then hooked them up to metal cables. With his hand on the lever, he peered directly at James.

"Not a scratch on her. Do I make myself clear?"

"Absolutely, man." He grinned broadly, showing brilliant white teeth. He turned to Alex. "Ready, Doc?"

"Can I go down with my eyes shut?" she asked.

Both men in unison yelled, "No!"

They started down.

It wasn't so bad. James gave good instructions on how to shift her weight and use her legs. Several rocks loosened under her boots and dropped her to her knees, but as Charles mentioned, it was a slope. Her fall was limited. If she told the people back in New York that she did a little mountain climbing on her vacation, they would never believe her.

James communicated with Charles via a radio clipped to his cop uniform. When they reached a wide flat area, he signaled an all-stop. He unhooked their harnesses.

"Not bad for a city girl," he said with a nice smile.

She looked up the slope. "How far down are we?"

"Roughly 300 feet. The animals did a number on our victim so I hope you got a strong stomach."

She touched his arm. "You realize I'm not a medical examiner."

He nodded. "The county only has one medical examiner, Doc. Usually a local doctor is recruited to help out—like we're doing with you." He led her to the body.

At first glance, she wasn't sure what James showed her. The body was mangled and hardly recognizable as a human skeleton. As she stood there and stared, a form came into focus. James dropped his backpack to the ground then reached in a compartment for latex gloves. He handed her a pair.

"I've already taken every conceivable photo of the body and scene," he said. "I have soil samples and collected everything in sight. I haven't moved the body at all. Just talk to me as you go, Doc."

Alexandra knelt alongside the body, not sure what to touch first. Half the flesh and muscle were gone, the rest dried up and stiff. "Definitely female," she said. "Internal organs are gone. Probably eaten. Several bones are missing. Multiple fractures for what remains." She turned the body. "Large muscle groups have been eaten. Several fractures of the spine. One hand is totally gone."

"I found that," he said. He reached into a plastic bag resting by the body. He pulled out a hand sealed in an evidence bag. "Also this." He held up another bag with the head.

She took the latter bag and examined the head. A young woman. Too young to die like this. "Massive skull fracture." She showed him. "A probable cause of death." She handed him the bag. When she turned back to the body, a shiny object caught her eye halfway buried in the dirt. She untangled it from the twisted clothing. "A necklace, James. Looks expensive."

He studied it with a deep frown forming on his handsome face. "Any ID under her?"

"Not that I see." She fingered the cloth of what

could have been a dress. "These aren't hiking clothes."

"No, they're not." He said it through tight teeth.

"Her shoes are missing."

"I found one. A high heel."

"So I suspected. I still see nylons on her legs." She sat back on her boots. "What now?"

He reached into his backpack. "We put her and her parts in a body bag. I will transport the bag and the evidence to the sheriff in the valley. He will call in the experts from Roanoke. Would you help me load her?"

While they watched the body bag inch its way up the mountain in a wire basket, James turned to her. "I'd appreciate if you kept quiet about this, Doc."

"No problem. It's not a great conversational piece. Is she a local?"

He shook his head. "No locals are reported missing. I have a good idea who she is but need proof before I say it. I'll give the sheriff what I have plus my suspicions. We'll go from there." He stared up at the wire basket. His blue eyes were intense, angry. "I studied forensics but never thought I'd use it on Billings Mountain. We've had our share of hikers getting hurt. They get lost; they get banged up, but never something like this."

Alex studied the slope. "That clearing up there isn't a lover's lane kind of thing, is it?"

"Yes." He said it softly, almost a whisper.

She shuddered. "Then you're talking murder, James."

He met her eyes. "Yes, I am."

****

Charles drove her back to the cabin. He hardly said two words along the way. His face resembled granite with eyes focused forward, unseeing. He was angry again, at the dead woman this time.

"I won't pretend to know you well, Charles, but I find it best not to jump to conclusions."

He looked at her. The anger eased to sadness. "I've lived on this mountain all my life, Alex. This has never happened before."

"Judging from the amount of decomposition, she's been there a long time. Hopefully, she'll turn up in a missing person's database."

He remained silent the rest of the way until he pulled up at the cabin. He turned to her. "Still going on your hike?"

"Oh, sure. I have the whole day ahead of me. I'm anxious to explore." Not to mention unravel her knotted nerves. She opened the truck door.

"Take your phone with you."

His tone surprised her. Commanding. No refusal accepted. "Yes, sir."

"And make sure it's on. If you have any difficulty at all, you call me, is that clear?"

She nodded stupidly. "Yes, sir."

That seemed to satisfy him. "Thanks for your help this morning."

That was it. Cut and dry. She watched the Red Baron drive away.

Chapter Six

Fall weather. A chill in the air, the sun hot and warming, the air crisp and clean. Perfect weather for a trek through the woods. Alex selected a path behind the cabin, picked up a large tree branch to use as a walking stick, and ventured uphill. She kept her pace slow and leisurely, pausing repeatedly to feel the forest around her. The higher she climbed the more vibrant the fall colors became. The valley below hung onto its blanket of green, but as her eyes scanned the surrounding mountaintops, fall colors glowed under a bright sun like a party hat on New Year's Eve. Just the tops of the mountains where the air blew cooler. Like here. Her path was golden or it was red, both color leaves crunching underfoot. Like a kid on holiday, she kicked everything in sight just to see it scatter.

After a few hours of exploring, her stomach complained about a lunch break. She stopped to listen to the surrounding forest. The sound of running water echoed through the trees off to the right. She left the trail and followed the sound until coming to...*a waterfall*! What a pleasant surprise! It was a small, picturesque scene straight off an artist's canvas with water flowing down a stone staircase into a clear pool. It created a stream that traveled lazily downhill. The perfect spot for a picnic.

While she sat on a boulder and ate, her mind

reflected on her adventure this morning. Murder. The word caused no emotion. City born and bred. Murder happened. Alex lost many patients on the table trying to prevent them from becoming a statistic. So who was this woman? Where was she from? If the clearing was a lover's lane, then she met someone. Perhaps a fight occurred, a confrontation, and her body tossed down the slope. A horrible way to go. Judging from the injuries, death came swiftly. She shuddered.

She just finished with a cup of coffee when the sound of crunching leaves made their way toward her. The footsteps were steady, in no hurry to get anywhere. Charles emerged from the forest a minute later, his face thoughtful. He paused to stare up a tree. A dead tree actually. He touched the bark like an arborist examining for disease then squatted to inspect the roots. The man gave every indication that he tended to an old friend.

"Is it really dead?" she asked.

Startled, he looked over and showed surprise. "I didn't see you there." He straightened up. "Yes, it's really dead. I'll have it cut down before it falls on someone." He approached. "Taking a break?"

"Yes. I have some coffee left. Want it?"

"No, thanks. I'm good. I see you found one of my favorite spots."

"Somehow, Charles, I believe you have a lot of favorite spots on this mountain."

No smile. No grin. Just a nod in acknowledgment. He sat on a nearby rock and picked up a twig. A sense of gloom hovered in his eyes. She attributed it to their morning adventure rather than the dead tree in the forest. It could be both for all she knew. "I didn't expect to see you so soon," she said. She poured the last of the coffee into her cup.

He shrugged his broad shoulders. "James went to the valley with the body. I can't do anything more so I'm doing my rounds." He paused, deep in thought. Then quickly as if to explain his presence, "I just came from one of the cabins. It's on the other side of that ridge." He pointed.

If he expected her to look, she didn't. She watched him instead as she sipped her coffee. A distinctive hormonal surge shot through her again. She hardly knew the man for such an intense reaction. Yet, here she sat with visions of a bed and this big man holding her. She shook it away. "How far up the mountain am I?"

"About two-thirds. You have enough daylight to make it to the top."

"And down again, I hope."

"And down again. Don't let me keep you."

"You're not." Alex was in no hurry to leave. She stared into the pool of water. Crystal clear. She touched it. Cold, too. New York used recycled water. From where, she dared not know.

"Where did you get the names for the cabins?" she asked. "I saw some very unusual names when I drove in. Bergamot was one."

"From the most prominent flower growing near it," he explained. "Yours is Rosebay Rhododendron. You should see the place in June and July. A mass of white and pink flowers everywhere. We're usually booked throughout spring and summer just for the flowers alone."

His voice spoke with pride, as if he planted every single seed. He treated the dead tree like an old friend.

He probably talked to all the flowers, too.

"You really love this mountain, don't you, Charles?"

"It's my home. It's where I grew up and more likely where I will die." He broke the twig into several small pieces and tossed them one by one into the water before continuing. "I've nothing else to compare it to. I had a happy enough childhood until my father became a tyrant. I escaped him by staying in the woods. It gave me a sense of freedom. I feel it to this day. You probably can't say that about the city."

She stifled a laugh. "Hardly. Freedom was getting home and bolting the door."

"How do you feel now?"

She thought about the answer for several long minutes. He didn't push. He just sat there with his gaze glued to her face.

"I guess I do feel a sense of freedom out here," she began. "There's a peacefulness about the mountain, and even this morning's discovery can't destroy it." A thoughtful pause. "I've worked so hard for so long that this one simple activity has me feeling...pleased. I can't explain it any better than that."

"I'd say you explained it well enough." His phone rang. He made a face but answered it. "Yes? And his reason was?" A heavy sigh. "All right. Tell him twenty minutes." He ended the connection. He growled at the phone. "I can't spend a decent few minutes with a beautiful woman without someone calling with a problem. I need to seriously reconsider this caretaker shit."

She smiled. "That was a nice compliment, Charles. Thank you."

"I meant every word of it." He tossed the last of the twig and stood to his feet. "Can I help you up?"

"A gesture to make up for my whirlwind thud on the porch?"

The man was way too serious. What would it take to put a smile on his face? Maybe he had no sense of humor. Some men were like that. She gulped the last of her coffee and threw everything into the backpack. She extended her hand. This seemed to please him for some reason.

"Enjoy your hike, Alexandra."

She watched him walk away. He gave a subtle glance over his shoulder before he disappeared into the trees.

A bright object caught her eye near the water's edge. She investigated with the use of her stick to knock the leaves off. A woman's scarf. A hot pink floral, once expensive, but now ruined. Lost on a hike no doubt. It didn't belong here. She tied it to the outside of her backpack as a reminder to toss it in the trash.

Alex continued her uphill climb until reaching the main road. She followed it the rest of the way just to see where it went. The road led to an overlook with an astounding view. As far as the eye could see, forests dotted with clumps of houses intermingled with more mountains. No sign of a big city anywhere. She stood there enthralled and vowed on the spot to return no matter how busy her schedule. She snapped a few photos with her cell phone to remind herself of that vow.

The sound of a heavy vehicle strained its way up the mountain. Seconds later, Harry's Tow Truck came around the bend. He stopped when he saw her and pulled over to the side.

"Hi!" he said jumping out. "Fancy meeting you here!" He strolled over. "You're carrying one big-ass of a staff, Doc. It's bigger than the both of us. You can fight off bears with that thing."

She met Harry when she stopped for gas the day of her arrival. He was one of the few men she could look directly in the eye since they stood nearly equal in height. His hair gave him an extra inch of height, however. He had it cropped short and sticking straight up. He wore wire-rimmed glasses which gave him a bookish appearance, and that contrasted sharply with his greasy coveralls. His hazel eyes were bright behind the glasses, and they studied her with appreciation.

"Hi, Harry. Where you heading?"

"Up the road a little ways. Zach Stewart's place. He can't get his car started. I'm not so sure I will either. It's a '63 Chevy, and parts are scarce. It's older than that tin can you're driving."

"Who's minding the garage?"

"My helper, Joey. I should call him my apprentice since I'm teaching him everything I know. Enjoying a hike?"

"Yes, I just had a nice lunch by a waterfall. How far to the top?"

He sat on the stone parapet before answering. His legs swung freely. "Not far. We have a one-way-in, one-way-out mountain road. People walk up to the top and expect to keep going down the other side. You'll see where it ends."

"Henrietta tells me one man owns this mountain."

"Yeah. He tends to keep to himself, not what we would call a recluse, just private." His phone rang. He checked caller ID then jumped off the parapet as if he was caught loafing. "It's Zach. He gets cranky if I don't run right up there." He put his phone away without answering. "Getting parts for Charles' truck is bad enough, but for Zach's—" He shook his head sadly. "Have a good hike, Doc." He ran to the truck and started off with a wave.

Harry knew she was a doctor. She never mentioned it to him so someone spread the word. She wasn't sure how she felt about it either. If Charles expressed bitterness toward her profession, others could feel the same. Just what she needed. The center of a hornet's nest. She continued uphill.

The asphalt road ended at a large circle. To the right of the circle stretched the entrance to a long circular driveway that led to an enormous white mansion high up on what appeared to be the top of the mountain. The structure of white brick glowed like a beacon despite clouds obscuring the sunlight. It had a wide, steep staircase leading to an open porch and ultimately to the front entrance of wide double doors. One side of the porch, the north, stretched away from the building partially suspended over the mountain. Glass encased the south side making a sunroom fit for a king.

She fell in love with the place. An old manor house without question. Probably late 19th Century. She envisioned horse-drawn carriages trotting up to the staircase. Women in sequined gowns would step carefully from the carriage, their gloved hands holding onto a male escort in tuxedo and top hat, all greeted by a properly starched butler at the door. No vehicles were in the drive now. No horse-drawn carriages either. Just one lone gardener with a weed-whacker trimming the edges of the lawn.

An elderly man walked out onto the porch and called to the gardener. He wore dress clothes and tie but no suit jacket. He conversed with the gardener then returned to the house. Neither noticed her.

Clouds? She looked skyward. What happened to that nice sunshine? She turned and headed back down the road.

A car whined its way uphill. She heard it before she saw it, the engine straining against gravity. It came around the bend seconds later. A black Camaro. With a redhead behind the wheel. A flaming redhead wearing dark Prada sunglasses. The woman from the general store. Alex waved to be polite. She received a glare that was unmistakable even from behind the sunglasses.

Miss Congeniality.

Not too many minutes later, Alex heard the car again. This time behind her heading downhill with more speed and definitely without the strain on the engine. Its speed increased as it rounded the curve. She glanced over her shoulder to confirm it.

The black Camaro *aiming straight toward her*!

Alex vaulted over the fender. She dropped with a thud and rolled as the wide tires spun on the loose stone shoulder. They squealed unmercifully, throwing dirt and stones in the process. The car disappeared before the dust cleared.

Alex jumped to her feet. And fell. Her knees wobbled like jelly. She wanted to run after the bitch and strangle her. She sat there instead, head on her knees, breathing hard. After several long minutes, she struggled to her feet and walked cautiously back to the road. Silence. With a curse more audible than muffled, she bent to retrieve her walking stick only to discover it smashed into four separate pieces.

Better the staff than me.

Heavy boots pounded the asphalt. Harry rounded the curve at a sprinter's speed. "Are you all right?" He reached her, breathless. "I heard tires squeal...whew!" He bent over to catch his breath. Then quickly, he caught her arm. "What happened?"

"Some woman in a black Camaro tried to run me over."

He started. "Sharon?"

"I don't know who she is. A redhead...in a black Camaro."

"Why would she do that?"

"How the hell would I know? Maybe she gets her jollies running over tourists. Look what she did to my staff!"

He took out his phone. "I'll call Charles."

"What the fig can Charles do?" She caught herself. "Sorry, Harry. Call James."

He studied her. "What's wrong with Charles?"

"Nothing. Just call James. Tell him to stop by my cabin." James should be the first call anyway. Why would Harry think to call Charles first? A police officer made it official, reports, inquiries, that sort of thing. What would Charles have done? Chop more wood? *The man in charge,* she thought solemnly. He had everyone trained.

"Walk with me to Zach's place. I'll drive you to the cabin."

She shook her head. "Thanks, but I'll hike down. The walk will calm my nerves."

63

She headed into the forest in case the bitch waited around the bend. Who the hell was she? Prada sunglasses were expensive, way beyond her own budget. The Camaro looked new. This Sharon was tall and gorgeous with a shape to make men drool. Billings' wife? A rich bitch with nothing better to do? It wouldn't surprise her one damn bit to find the thought to be true.

Alex followed a path that led to another waterfall, smaller than the first but nonetheless welcoming. She used the cold water to rinse her face and hands, pissed as all get-out to see her hands still shaking.

Goddamn bitch. She continued downhill.

The path took her past the remains of an old stone house. Not much left of it. One corner and a doorway. Part of a chimney. Part of a wall. A large tree trunk about three feet in diameter laid smack through the center of it, its core rotted and hollow. Two relics forgotten by time.

She moved on.

She realized with a start that fog surrounded her. She had been so preoccupied with the redhead that she failed to notice the change in the atmosphere. Like a heavy cloud, it rolled in thick and fast, obscuring the path and the forest beyond. She stopped, awestruck by all the white, feeling smothered, totally blinded by this dense, eerie fog.

What the hell kind of day am I having here? Maybe she should have stayed in that king sized bed...no, maybe she should have stayed in New York holed up in her apartment.

Oh, who was she kidding? She wanted out of New York to experience something new. But not a day like this. How the hell was she supposed to see? Her cell phone rang. She jumped from the sound as it echoed and bounced around the trees. A flood of relief swept through her when she saw the caller ID.

"Where are you?" Charles asked.

"Right smack in the middle of this fog. I'm heading downhill on a path that took me past an old stone house."

"With a tree through it? Then I know exactly where you are. Do you want me to come and get you?"

"Charles, I would be thrilled."

"Sit tight. I'll be there in five minutes."

Too long. Too long. Panic set in. She closed her eyes to shut out the fog.

"Alex!"

Thank God. "Over here!"

This big looming shadow pushed its way through the thick mist. He looked as nonchalant as usual as if he were out for a stroll. She never saw a more wonderful sight. She almost jumped into his arms. "You're looking out for me, Charles."

"You're new here. Fog comes in fast on these mountains. Next time, you'll know to get yourself on the road. You can follow asphalt better than a dirt path. Stay behind me." They walked a mere dozen feet when panic overwhelmed her again. *She just could not see*!

"Charles—" Her voice cracked.

His hand reached back and slipped over hers. The touch of his skin created an extraordinary sense of calm. She never felt anything like it. It told her that everything was going to be all right. He gave her fingers an affectionate squeeze as he guided her out of the woods.

Chapter Seven

The midget in the shadow of the giant again. Strength flowed through that strong, callused hand. It suppressed her panic and erased every last bit of apprehension. Alex didn't care that she couldn't see. She didn't care if the black Camaro sat lurking around the bend. Charles was here, and Charles was holding her hand.

It felt pretty damn good.

"I'll give you a lift back," he said as they approached the Red Baron. She removed her backpack and tossed it in the bed of the truck. She jumped into the passenger seat while he settled behind the wheel. "Have a good hike?" he asked.

"Yes, despite the fog. Between the slope and the hike, I'm afraid my calves will cramp up tonight."

His lips pursed as he scanned her from head to toe. "You look like you took a spill." He reached over and pulled several pine needles out of her hair.

"More like a roll." She had not bothered with her hair since her flying leap. She checked for rips and tears but never a thought to her head. She shook it now. "Any more?"

The intensity in his gaze made her wonder if some of her hair fell out. She checked her lap anyway.

"One more." He said it softly while taking the pine needle from the back of her head. His expression grew shuttered as he started the truck. "This fog will be with us till morning. I suggest you take a nice warm shower and relax. It will help your calves."

The road proved no better than the forest. The truck cut through a thick mist that made it virtually impossible to see. He drove as if the fog didn't exist.

"I have never experienced fog so thick," she said with a slight gasp. She looked out the side window. Nothing but shadows.

"We're used to it. We have a lot of trouble with our guests when the fog rolls in. Sometimes—"

He slammed on the brakes. Her heart jumped into her throat as she jerked against the seatbelt then quickly jerked back. He threw the gearshift into reverse, creating another jerk.

Red flashing lights reflected off the surrounding fog, familiar flashing lights coming from a driveway on her right.

"No one called me," he said in a half mumble. "Would you mind if we stop?"

"Of course not. Where are we?"

"This is Mrs. O'Reilly's house. The lady is in her 80's so I hope nothing serious is going on." He turned in. "She's watching her grandson while her son and daughter-in-law attend an out-of-state wedding. I don't want you to get involved. Just stay in the truck."

"All right." No argument there.

Charles maneuvered the Red Baron down a dirt drive and pulled alongside an ambulance. From what Alex could tell, the old woman looked just fine. A rotund woman she was, complete with red cheeks and round head. A little boy of perhaps ten stood next to her crying his eyes out. She talked feverishly to two ambulance men, her pudgy arms flaring, finger pointing in the direction of the backyard. As Charles approached, an immediate calming effect took hold. A deep discussion followed. Then, all five of them walked further down the drive and disappeared into the fog.

If the ambulance wasn't for the old woman, and it wasn't for the boy, then a third party hid somewhere in the fog. Curiosity got the best of her. Alex stepped out of the truck.

A commotion from the direction of the backyard drew her. She approached slowly, well aware of her intrusion. The little boy still wailed, but now he draped himself over a big brown Newfoundland. His mannerism suggested protection, a go-away-don't-touch-him posture. The four adults stood there and watched.

The dog looked seriously ill. It laid on its belly panting horribly, mouth ajar. Saliva dangled from his lips in a disgusting long string and coated his forepaws. His eyes were glassy and tired. She heard their conversation now.

"We'll take him to the vet if you want," one crewman said, "but it's a long ride in this fog. The ambulance won't be available if a real emergency comes up."

"This *is* an emergency!" the little boy wailed. He jumped to his feet to tug on Charles' arm. "Make them take him!"

"I think it's rabies myself," the other crewman said. "We should put the dog out of its misery. What do you think, Charles?"

Alex marveled at how everyone turned toward Charles for advice, as if he had all the answers. The old woman immediately calmed when he approached, just like Alex did in the forest. The little boy made it sound as if Charles had the final say and could override everyone's decision. Now, the crewman asked for his opinion. Even Harry wanted to call him first. What the hell was going on here? Was Charles more than a caretaker on this mountain? If so, who or what was he?

Her step forward to hear his reply caught the old woman's attention.

"You're Dr. Colter, aren't you? I'm Anita O'Reilly. This is my grandson, Michael. Will you tell these hardheaded men that this dog doesn't have rabies?"

"I'm afraid I know very little about rabies," Alex answered.

The little boy came running, nearly stumbling on a clump of grass. "You gotta save Bluto!" he pleaded. "He's my best friend in the whole world!"

Charles stood watching her. Alex heard his mental reprimand. *You should have stayed in the truck.* Like any woman, she was nosy as hell. "All right, Michael, take me to Bluto."

Charles stepped in her path. "I wouldn't," he said sternly. "If the dog has rabies—"

"Bluto does not have rabies!" the boy cried.

Alex doubted if Michael would know rabies when he saw it, but she took his side anyway. "I'll be careful."

Michael led her to his friend.

Poor Bluto. His tongue hung out to the side useless and dry despite all the saliva dripping. Tears filled his eyes, and a faint cry rolled out of his throat. She got down on her knees to study him. "How long has he been like this?" she asked Michael.

"Only a few minutes."

Mrs. O'Reilly stepped in. "A few hours, Michael. You must be specific when talking to a doctor."

"When did it start?" Alex asked her.

"Well, he was fine all morning. Then Michael and I went inside for lunch. Bluto stayed out here. We found him like this when we came out."

"Does anyone have a flashlight?" Alex asked.

"We do." A crewman ran to his rig.

"And a pair of gloves!" she called.

He returned with the gloves and a large black flashlight, the kind long enough to use like a club. Alex removed her jacket, rolled up her sweatshirt sleeves, then put on the gloves. She positioned herself directly in front of Bluto to take a good look inside his opened mouth. The problem was obvious. "It's not rabies," she told everyone. "Bluto has something jamming his jaw open."

"I told them it wasn't rabies!" Michael dropped onto his knees and looked at her hopefully. "Can you get it out?"

"I'm going to try." She turned to the ambulance crew. "Do you guys carry a forceps?"

"No, ma'am."

Life was never easy. "Charles, do you have leather gloves with you?"

"In my truck. Why?"

"I want you to put them on and help me."

He stared. "*Me*!"

"Yes, you. I want you to straddle Bluto and hold his head between your knees. With your gloves on, I want you to hold the dog's jaw open."

70

"What are you going to do?" he asked with suspicion.

"I'm going to reach down his throat and pull out whatever is in there."

"You are not!"

"If I don't, Bluto will dehydrate and die. Michael, when did Bluto get his last rabies shot?"

"This summer. Mom and I took him to the vet in the valley."

Alex turned back to Charles. "See? Let's try it."

"I don't want you to get hurt."

"That's why you are going to hold his jaw open. I trust you enough not to let go. Just don't rip his jaw apart."

Charles eyed her warily. He stared down at the dog then back at her. He wasn't going to win this one. She was hardheaded and determined when it came to being a doctor even if she didn't know a damn thing about animals.

"All right, I'll get my gloves."

Alex turned to Mrs. O'Reilly. "Do you have a bunch of old towels we can use?"

"Absolutely." She hurried into the house.

"What am I supposed to do?" Michael asked.

"You have to stay right alongside me so Bluto sees you. Your job is to keep him calm."

"I can do that."

Mrs. O'Reilly returned with the towels. Alex handed them to Michael. "It's your job to clean him, too."

With her surgical team in place, Alex looked up into a pair of worried eyes. The caretaker. *Her* caretaker. A nice warm feeling flowed under her skin

71

when their eyes met.

"I might do some serious damage to this dog if he hurts you," he said. The words came out as a muttered growl.

"You can't hurt Bluto. Michael will be very upset."

"Yeah!" Michael agreed.

"Bluto will resist us," she told them. "Michael, keep talking to him. Charles, try to keep his head still without crushing his skull between your knees. I have to get in and remove this thing without pushing it further down his throat. Everyone ready?"

They were. Alex nodded at Charles. He grabbed hold of Bluto's jaw. She shoved her hand in fairly certain how far to reach. She felt the object and drew it out. Once clear, Charles released his grip, and Bluto's jaw snapped shut.

Michael was a happy little boy.

Alex stood to her feet to a round of applause. Mrs. O'Reilly crushed Alex against her large, soft bosom in a hug that squeezed the air out in a huff. When Alex could get a breath in, she said, "Mrs. O'Reilly—"

"Say no more, dear. Come into the kitchen and wash."

Alex followed her into the house, quickly torn off her saliva-covered gloves and washed. She also washed what she yanked out of Bluto's mouth. It was a piece of rusty metal.

"Bluto needs to be checked out by the vet," she told her. "He may have damage to the roof of his mouth."

"I'll make arrangements to take a ride into the valley tomorrow—unless you think we need to go today."

"I wouldn't take a chance in this fog. Wait until tomorrow. If he doesn't eat his dinner, you'll know his mouth hurts. Take this piece of metal with you."

"I want to pay you."

"Absolutely not."

"But you're a guest on this mountain. You didn't have to do this. Tell her, Charles."

Charles stood right behind her. She never heard him enter the kitchen. He took her hand and inspected it. His touch was gentle, almost a caress. It surprised her that a man with such strength could touch with such tenderness. She found herself staring at him in awe.

"Not a scratch," he said softly. He released her hand. "She is a woman who makes up her own mind, Mrs. O'Reilly."

Yes, I am, she thought proudly.

"Well then, that's settled."

"How did you know who I was?" Alex asked.

Clear gray eyes twinkled. "Henrietta described you as a goddess. After meeting you, I have to agree." She grabbed Alex's hand and gave it a good shake. "I'm so glad to meet you, Dr. Colter. You're welcome to stop by any time."

As Charles drove, Alex threw a few discreet glances in his direction only to see him doing the same to her. Something electric shot around in the truck cab. When their eyes met, sparks flew. It startled her enough to make her eyes blink. This never happened before with any man. Actually, she never took the time to notice.

"I feel stunned," she said finally. "I live in a city with millions of people, and yet I'm so alone. Here, people know me before I'm introduced. Do you realize

I don't even know my neighbors in my apartment building?"

"We're a small community," he explained. "Word travels fast. It will travel even faster after this."

"I didn't do anything special."

"That's where you're wrong, Alex. We have doctors who rent our cabins, male and female. Quite a few walk around with their nose in the air. I doubt they would have bothered with that dog like you did." He gave her a quick, sweeping glance. "You really can't resist helping people, can you? Even a little boy with a dog."

She shrugged. "Ever since I was a kid, I enjoyed helping people. I saved my first life when I was ten. A man dropped dead in the store. I remembered CPR from a TV show so I pumped on his chest until he gasped. It was a great feeling. I knew then that I wanted to be a doctor. I'd do it for nothing if I didn't have huge bills to pay."

"Payment in chickens, you mean?"

"Something like that. Besides, I'm a sucker for crying little boys. You would have done the same thing."

"Don't be so sure. I was ready to go home and get my gun."

Her mouth fell open. The sparkle in his eyes slapped it shut. "Liar." She chuckled softly. "I get a lot of joy helping people. It's what pushed me to become a doctor. My parents nearly had a stroke when I told them I wanted to go to med school. We didn't have any money. So I knew it was entirely up to me."

"You must have made them very proud."

She shook her head sadly. "They were both dead

before I finished my first year."

Silence fell in the cab. She knew he watched her, and he drove noticeably slower as his gaze pierced into her soul.

"Why are you alone, Alex? I mean, really alone?"

It took a few moments to answer. The man was too damn easy to talk to, and she wasn't sure how much of herself to reveal. He took her hand, as if contact lowered her guard. His hand was callused against her soft skin. A man's hand, a hand used to hard work. It did lower her guard, unfortunately. "I've been alone all my life, Charles. It doesn't bother me anymore."

"I don't believe that for one second. You've been alone for so long, you accept it as the norm. I also see you as blinded by this single-minded obsession of being a great doctor. You put others needs before your own. That's why you live your life alone because your eyes aren't open to the possibilities. When are you going to look out for your own needs, Alex?"

Her eyes flashed. "You don't know anything about me."

"Yeah, well, I observe. Why aren't you in a relationship?"

She looked at him squarely. "That is none of your business."

He eyed her knowingly. "No man in his right mind would let a beautiful woman like you come all the way down here by herself."

"I don't let any man control me."

That shut him up. Unfortunately, he hit a raw nerve. She sighed heavily. "I'm not in a relationship, Charles. I've never been close enough to a man to ask him to stay. I doubt if I ever will. So, yeah, I live alone and I love my job. I'm the loudest patient advocate in the hospital, and I'll fight whoever gets in my way."

"Who will fight for you, Alex?"

The man put a stake straight into her heart. She had no one to come to her rescue, no one to call, no one to count on. She avoided eye contact by staring out the side window.

He turned the truck sharply. "Sorry. Almost missed your road."

When he pulled up to the cabin, she barely made out the shadow of the roof in the fog. He stopped her from opening the door.

"I'm sorry," he said softly.

She stared out into the fog. "Truth hurts."

"I said those exact same words to you yesterday."

So he did. It brought out a little smile. "I've no one to fight for me, Charles. It's a reality I've had to face for a long time. I guess that's why I'm such a loud patient advocate." She shook herself. "Where do you live?"

He looked at her cautiously. "Up the road a little ways. Why did you say you trusted me?"

He changed the subject as quickly as she did. They could be on the same wavelength, which was frightening. She stepped out. "Because I do."

"Why? You hardly know me."

"I don't understand it either. It's just a strong feeling that you won't let anything happen to me. I hope I'm not wrong."

One corner of his lip twitched. "No, you're not wrong."

The man saw through her faster than wind through a screen. She hated vulnerability. It was the kiss of death on the inner city streets. It could be the kiss of death here on this mountain, too. "Thanks for the rescue." She grabbed the backpack from the bed of the truck.

"Alex."

His tone surprised her. It stopped her from closing the truck door. "What?"

"Where'd you get that scarf?"

She looked down at the dirty piece of silk dangling from her backpack. "I found it on the trail. It's ruined. I'm going to toss it in the trash. Do you want it?"

"Yes, I do."

She undid it and handed it to him. "It's not your color, you know."

No smile. No glint of humor. Just that damn piece of granite again. "I have lipstick if you want to try that, too."

His head snapped toward her, but she stood with a sweet smile on her lips. His eyes turned into slits. "Wise ass. Tell me where you found it."

She told him. "I guess you know who it belongs to."

"Yes. Don't let the fog deter you from hiking again."

He waited until she opened the door to the cabin before speeding away.

Chapter Eight

Alex fell into bed early, utterly exhausted. By morning, she could barely swing her legs off the mattress. At least she'd slept this time. Charles drifted into her mind briefly when she first shut her eyes. Exhaustion kept him away after that.

A little after the noon hour, Alex took her second cup of coffee out to the bench by the cliff and put her feet up. Her usual position. She loved this bench. She loved sitting with a cup of coffee watching the picturesque landscape below. The hawk circled above her. She raised her cup in a gesture of salute to say hello. She could sit for hours and suck in the peacefulness of her surroundings.

She wished she had enough money to buy the damn place.

A rustling in the bushes snapped her ears to attention. The red moved before the yellow. "Hi, Lucy. Come out and sit with me."

The little blonde crept out of the bushes with a great deal of hesitation, her red Elmo doll clutched tightly to her chest. Those startling blue eyes stared wide with curiosity.

"Come sit with me," Alex repeated and patted the bench. "I could use some company."

Lucy approached gingerly. She exhibited no fear, but her uncertainty showed with every step. She sat at the opposite end of the bench, not brave enough to sit close. Her eyes watched and waited.

"How old are you?"

Lucy held up five fingers.

"Wow! Five years old! I don't have enough fingers and toes to count on to tell you how old I am."

A faint giggle rose from the girl's throat.

A sound from Lucy! Not a word but definitely a sound.

"Can we be friends, Lucy?"

She nodded vigorously.

"I'm glad because I need a friend right now, and I will say this only to a friend. Can I tell you a secret? Charles had to rescue me from the fog yesterday. It was pretty scary. I don't think I have ever been so scared. Have you ever been scared?"

Another nod but a more hesitant one. Her cute face grew thoughtful.

"I couldn't see where I was, and I had to stand there and wait for Charles. I was so scared, I almost cried. You won't tell anyone, will you?"

Lucy shook her head.

"That's good because friends are supposed to talk to each other. Otherwise, they wouldn't be very good friends. You'll keep my secret? And if you tell me anything, I will keep it a secret, too. Is it a deal?"

Lucy nodded. She sat swinging her legs, Elmo on her lap. She looked shy and bashful and so cute.

"Shall we make our friendship official, Lucy?" Alex held up her little finger. "You have to hook your finger in mine."

No hesitation this time. She wiggled across the bench to hook her little finger. They sealed the pact.

She did not attempt to move away afterwards. She sat swinging her legs, her eyes full of anticipation. Of what, Alex wasn't sure. She had little experience entertaining children.

"Does Henrietta know you're here?"

In answer, Lucy slid off the bench and grabbed Alex's hand. She tugged and pointed toward the path.

"You want me to walk you home? Sure, I'll do that. Let me put my cup in the sink, and we'll be off."

Alex did more than put her cup in the sink. She grabbed her cell phone. After yesterday's adventure, she made a vow never to leave it behind.

Alex and Lucy walked hand-in-hand down the path, through the tunnel, and over the wooden bridge. Lucy's little hand held on firmly, pulling from time to time to hurry Alex along. She pulled her heartstrings, too. This little girl remained silent for a reason, and Alex would not be on Billings Mountain long enough to find out why. When they reached the general store, Lucy tugged and led the way around the back toward a cottage.

It was an enchanting little place, constructed entirely in brown stones with a cedar-shingled roof and red wooden shutters. A two-foot high stone parapet separated it from the back of the general store. The Red Baron sat parked near it along with the Billings Mountain police cruiser. The latter piqued her interest, but Lucy's face showed eagerness, not concern, and definitely not alarm. Lucy tugged her toward the back of the cottage.

Alex stopped her. "Lucy, I can't enter a house uninvited." Lucy tugged and insisted. Alex resisted.

"It's about time you two showed up," said a sultry

voice. Henrietta stood halfway out the back door. "I told Lucy she could invite a friend to her party. When she bolted out of here, I had a feeling she was going for you. Come on in."

"What party?"

"It's Lucy's birthday today. She just turned five. We're having coffee and cake."

"Who's minding the store?"

"Honey, if I want to close the store for a few hours, I do so. Now, get your pretty butt in here."

Lucy pulled Alex toward the door and into the house. They walked directly into a small kitchen where two women Henrietta's age sat at a table decorated with cake and candles. Henrietta introduced them, but their names went right over her head. The two women were nondescript. They looked nearly identical because of short curly gray hair. Alex's attention riveted instead on the two men standing on opposite sides of the refrigerator.

The contrast between them was striking. While Charles resembled Darth Vader in casuals with a smoldering look plastered all over his face, James brightened the room like a ray of sunshine with blue eyes sparkling. Placed side-by-side, they looked about the same age and stood nearly the same height. Weight-wise, Charles won. His broad chest and thick arms made James look trim and svelte in his well-fitted police uniform. One comparison eluded her, however. James smiled. Charles did not. She had yet to see his teeth. Even now, his face expressed a seriousness more fit for a funeral than a birthday party. He may as well be Darth Vader, she told herself. That man never smiled either. One common detail struck her, however. These two handsome men eyed her as if she stood there butt naked.

"All right, everybody!" Henrietta clapped her hands. "Time to light the candles!"

A chorus of "Happy Birthday" followed, and Lucy blew out her candles. Alex went to sit next to one of the older women, but Henrietta grabbed her shoulders and guided her toward another chair. She literally pushed Alex down onto the seat then leaned over to whisper in her ear. "Better view this way, dear."

Alex looked up to see she faced Charles and James, both of whom watched with a great deal of interest. Lucy sat on one side, Henrietta on the other. Charles and James remained standing.

The conversation was light and cheerful, more gossipy than anything else. One girl had a baby—her fourth. Someone else built an addition onto his house. James told stories that made everyone laugh. Charles said very little. Clearly, James had the more outgoing personality, and the women loved it. Yet, despite a growing interest in the handsome cop, Alex's gaze constantly drifted to the man nearby. Every time their eyes met, they locked in unison. He had an unmistakable pull on her, like a magnet attracting its mate. Each time it got harder to pull away. As before in the truck cab, she didn't understand the feelings he stirred in her then. She certainly didn't understand them now.

During the second round of coffee, Henrietta boldly announced, "Alexandra is a doctor, everyone. A surgeon. Can you imagine waking up from surgery and seeing this face leaning over you?"

"I'd think I died and went to heaven," James said

with an exaggerated sigh.

Everyone laughed. Except Charles. His brows came together in a frown and stayed that way.

"I hear she also operates on dogs." This from the woman named Barbara.

"No, no," Alex corrected. "It had a piece of metal stuck in his throat. I wouldn't have touched him without Charles there. He held the dog's jaw open for me."

All eyes shifted to Charles who looked slightly uncomfortable.

"Now you're a medical assistant," James said while slapping his friend's shoulder.

Charles found no humor in that either.

"I wonder why Mrs. O'Reilly didn't call me." James pondered. "I would have jumped at the chance to be the doctor's assistant."

Charles shot him a black look.

"Alexandra's name is all over the internet," Henrietta said. "Sorry, dear, I couldn't resist looking you up. You have quite a reputation in New York. They claim you are the promising young surgeon of the decade. Quite a compliment. I must admit, you photograph well."

Alex's cheeks flushed. "New York Presbyterian posted that photo. It will probably stay on the net long after I'm old and gray." She put more cream in her coffee.

She wondered how Charles came to the conclusion of her single-minded obsession about her work. This was her answer. He looked her up on the internet, saw all the positive reviews, and yes, how they labeled her as an up-and-coming surgeon. That was hospital press, though, and he shouldn't judge her on that alone. It wasn't fair.

She glanced up at him to meet his gaze. Yes, that was the answer. He just told her so, and she surprised herself that she actually read it on his face so easily. But she wasn't obsessed with work. She was obsessed with paying off her debt. He needed to understand the difference.

"I think you'll look gorgeous at any age," James said. "I'll have to go home and take a look at it, maybe use the photo as my wallpaper. Then I can drool every time I turn on my computer."

Charles suddenly excused himself and left, looking like a rumbling thundercloud. James' blue eyes twinkled. "I guess it's time I take off, too. I'll give him a head start just in case he's lurking by the back door waiting to bash my head in. Ladies, always a pleasure." He gave Lucy a kiss on her blonde head, winked at Alex, then left. All three women immediately leaned forward on the table.

"I can't believe what we just witnessed!" Henrietta said with a gasp. She grabbed Alex's hand. "You must realize, Alexandra, that very few single women pass through here. Charles and James are best friends and look what happened."

Alex finished the last of her cake. "What happened?"

All three women stared. The one named Marge found her voice first. She turned to Henrietta. "Is she joking?"

"It didn't sound like it." Henrietta leaned over to stare into Alex's face. "You really don't know what happened?"

"From your insinuations, I assume something went

right over my head."

"Honey, not only did it go over your head, but it thumped you on the way out. No wonder you're still single. You wouldn't know a flirt unless a man flashed a neon sign."

Uh-oh! *That missing gene again.* "Who was flirting?" She asked it sheepishly.

No one answered. They only stared.

Henrietta shook herself. "James, dear, from the second you stepped through the door. It infuriated Charles. The man became absolutely livid. You could practically see the steam rise from his collar. I'm sure you saw it."

"Well, no. And if you're telling me that the two of them behaved like dogs in heat, then that's too bad."

"For your information," Marge said, "James was going out of his way to make Charles jealous."

"Why?"

"Oh, God!" Marge put her head in her hands. "I've heard of brainy women not having a clue, but I thought it was made-up movie stuff."

Henrietta laughed. "Alexandra Colter, you are the most refreshing woman to pass through here in a long time. All right, ladies, we're changing the subject."

"Good. I'll start," Alex said eagerly. A little too eagerly when she thought about it. "When I was out hiking yesterday, I came to a wonderful white manor house. Who does it belong to?"

"That's the Billings house," Henrietta said. She poured more coffee into their cups while Lucy and Alex took a second piece of cake. "You, of course, don't know the history of Billings Mountain so I will tell you. The Billings family staked a claim on this mountain way back in the 1820's. They made their fortune in coal and lumber, both businesses sold off somewhere in the 1950's. The family lives on invested money today, which is substantial. There are approximately 250 of us who live on this mountain, some third and fourth generation. We are a small community where everyone knows their neighbor, and we help the other out when necessary. We own our homes, but we pay rent to the Billings estate for the land it sits on, similar to real estate taxes. We have no local government. Any disputes are brought before Mr. Billings for discussion. James is our law enforcement officer. He has direct connections to the sheriff in the valley. We wouldn't have him if it weren't for the outsiders who come up here to cause trouble. James is paid with our rent money, as are our two schoolteachers, fire and ambulance equipment, trash pickup, everything you expect taxes to cover. The seven cabins were put up to boost our small economy. The money they earn goes into a fund to help whoever might need it or to purchase something special like the basketball court at the elementary school. How the money is used is decided by a committee of which H.C. Billings has no part. Anything else, ladies?"

"The committee decided to expand to ten cabins," Barbara said. "There are plans for a small café. A lot of our guests want a place to stop and eat."

"I can relate to that," Alex said. "However, mathematically, you can't afford that list of expenses unless Billings has the rent real high. You haven't even touched the subject of a school budget."

Henrietta's brown eyes twinkled. "That's correct, dear. The man is extraordinarily wealthy. Lucky for us, he is not a greedy man. We can afford to live here without hardship."

"It's not exciting enough for the young people," Marge said while putting an overabundance of sugar into her coffee. "They go to high school in the valley. After they graduate, they usually pack up and move away. Most live where the jobs are."

"Which isn't Billings Mountain," Barbara continued, "but we like it here. We do things as a community."

"Speaking of which," Henrietta said, "there's a star party tomorrow night at the elementary school. Everyone's invited, guests included. Charles runs it. He's the one with all the knowledge about the stars and planets. He sets up his telescopes, and everyone gets a chance to look through them."

"It's a learning experience for the kids," Marge said.

"Adults, too," Barbara interjected. "I always learn something new every time we have the party."

Lucy tugged eagerly on Alex's sleeve. Henrietta looked over at her and smiled. "Lucy wants you to come, don't you, Lucy?"

The little blonde head nodded.

Alex began to feel slightly stunned by all the attention. Her life in New York was eat, work, sleep. Day after day. Week after week. A date was rare. Rarer still was a party. Of course, a vacation meant having new experiences, and she definitely had a growing list. Even more puzzling, she came onto Billings Mountain with the intention of spending the week in solitude. Every day, something new popped up. Like now. "All right. I have no idea what I'm getting into, but I'll come. What time?"

The women looked at her as if she suddenly spoke a foreign language. Henrietta patted her arm. "Dark, of course. You can't see stars until it gets dark."

"Brains and no clue," Marge murmured.

"It's weather dependent," Henrietta continued. "The forecast is for clear so we're keeping our fingers crossed."

"Should I bring anything?"

"Warm clothing. The mountain gets pretty cold at night. If you hear a weather forecast, it's usually for temperatures in the valley. Subtract ten degrees for up here. I will supply coffee and hot chocolate. We usually have a pretty good time."

"Then I guess we have a date at the elementary school," Alex said to Lucy. "Happy birthday, little one. Thank you for inviting me. I will see you tomorrow night."

Lucy grabbed hold of her neck and jerked her down to plant a kiss on her cheek. Alex returned the kiss along with a hug then stood to her feet. "Ladies, it's been a pleasure sharing coffee and cake with you."

Alexandra left, mindful that she would be the topic of discussion for three older women as soon as she shut the door.

Chapter Nine

Charles sat waiting on the front porch the next morning. Alex never heard him drive in and had no idea how long he had been waiting. She stopped when she saw him, hesitant as to why he showed up. He turned when she stepped out. He looked tired and drawn. Dirt covered his blue jeans and flannel shirt. They were the same clothes he wore at the birthday party.

"Can we prevail ourselves of your services again, doctor?" He said it with a hint of despair.

She sat next to him on the porch. "Please don't tell me you found another body."

He stared at the forest opposite, unmoving. "That is exactly what happened. James needs you again. *We* need you again."

She watched two chipmunks chase each other around the truck tires. The serenity they offered was shattered by the reality of Charles' words. "Maybe you should call in the state police. Obviously, something serious is going on."

"It's serious all right, and I can't tell you how grateful I am to have you here. Please." His eyes pleaded. His voice shook. The man bordered on stress overload, and she wondered why he took it so personal.

She nodded and stood to her feet. "One minute." She went into the cabin to grab her cell phone and key. Charles stood to his feet when she reemerged. "I might ask for a refund, you know."

They drove off toward the main road.

There was no mountain climbing this time, for which she was very thankful. She asked him that question before she stepped into the truck. Charles eventually turned off the asphalt road and drove the Red Baron down a small service road until it could go no further. He parked alongside the police cruiser, and together, they walked into the forest.

She heard the waterfall a few minutes later. Her gut told her they were heading that way. It was where she uncovered the scarf.

"It took us a while to find the grave," he said solemnly. "We knew it couldn't be close to the trail. With the amount of hikers we get up here, I'm surprised it stayed hidden so long. This way."

They followed the small stream downhill for perhaps a hundred feet before turning left. They finally reached James, who busily labeled evidence packets. He looked up as they approached. "Morning, Doc." No smile came to his lips. Like Charles, he looked tired and overwrought.

Alex grabbed a pair of gloves from his backpack and went directly to the body.

The murderer had buried this one. The men had already removed the dirt and revealed a shallow grave about a foot deep. Its position showed haste without concern. She knelt alongside. James knelt opposite.

"Definitely not what I would call a proper burial," she began. "Another female." A fact more apparent than the first body. "Clothes are still intact. No dirt in her mouth or nostrils so she was dead before being buried. No evidence of trauma or broken bones anteriorly. Help me turn her, James."

For some reason, she expected to find the massive skull fracture. "This head wound is consistent with the first victim," she said thoughtfully, "and nearly identical in location." They turned her back. "At least these aren't party clothes. She's dressed for summertime hiking with lightweight shirt and pants." She lifted some clothing. "This body is more intact. No blood on the front of the clothes, just the back where the head wound is. Otherwise, I don't see any evidence of another injury." She sat back on her boots, looked around, and realized with a start that Charles was no longer with them. "Where'd Charles go?"

"He's not handling this well, Alex. This has never happened up here on Billings Mountain. When he handed me the scarf, I thought the big guy would break down right in front of me."

"You know her?"

"Yes." He said it through tight teeth. "I knew the first victim, too." His eyes locked onto hers. "There's a third somewhere."

Alex sucked in a breath so hard and fast, she swore dry leaves sucked straight into her throat. She went into a coughing fit.

"Sorry, I thought you should know."

"So I can get the hell off this mountain? Hell, yeah, I'll pack and leave tonight!"

James reached to grab her arm, realized he had gloves on, and retracted. "I don't want you to leave, Alex. I need your help. Someone on this mountain committed these murders."

"You don't know that for sure. It could be an outsider coming up here. You said no locals were missing, right? Then that means these women were visitors—or guests." She shuddered. "There's no way I can help you, James. I'm not cut out for this kind of stuff."

"You're a doctor with a good head on your shoulders. I have a strange feeling you don't scare easily. You're going to help me catch this killer."

She stared at him. "How?"

"By being here, by talking to people, listening. Besides, you're the one person I know for sure is innocent." He stood to his feet and took out a body bag. They loaded the body. When they finished, he looked down at her, his face serious. "Don't mention the bodies, Alex. Charles and I are keeping it under wraps. The killer must not know that we found them."

They both tore off their latex gloves.

"How do you know there's a third, James?"

He gathered up his little evidence packets before answering. "Because a third woman disappeared just like these two. I can't explain any more than that. It will reveal too much." He placed the packets into a large manila envelope. "The coroner should confirm a few of my suspicions, but without proof, I won't get anywhere." He placed everything into his backpack and closed it up. "You won't be able to carry the body bag so I'll get Charles back here. He's probably waiting by the truck. Follow me." He hoisted his backpack over one shoulder.

"Wait, James." She grabbed his arm. "Charles met me at the waterfall. He came up through these woods to reach it. If he knows every square inch of the mountain, why hasn't he found the grave before this?"

"I don't know," he said softly. "He would have

been the one to see it when it was fresh."

Their eyes locked. Her gut screamed *No!* Her brain said otherwise. Intellect and heart collided. Neither won.

"Harry told me what happened on the road," he said. "I want to apologize for not getting back to you sooner, but these two bodies took precedence. I managed to talk to Sharon, however. She claims she lost control around the curve. Are there any witnesses?"

Sharon's word against hers. A local versus a visitor. Great. She shook her head. "Is she Billings' wife?"

He started. "What made you think that?"

"You know, rich bitch. That sort of thing."

"She'd like to be Billings' wife, but she isn't. She's one of our school teachers." He scratched his neck. "I wrote up the incident, but a lot of drivers lose control around our curves. It won't hold up in court, Alex."

The story of her life. A day late, a dollar short. Every cliché in the book. A crazy woman attempted to rearrange her pelvis, and not a damn shred of proof that it was intentional.

"If she claims it was an accident, why didn't she stop to see if I was all right? I saw her laughing at me, James."

He looked at her steadily but said nothing. She got the distinct feeling that he hid something from her. This friggin' mountain was full of secrets. Maybe she should just pack up and leave.

"Stay, Alex," he said as if reading her mind.

She debated telling him to go suck an egg. Instead, she said, "Yeah, I'll finish out my week." It could be the worst mistake of her life.

James led the way back through the woods. When they reached the waterfall, she stopped. "I think I'll walk to the cabin," she said.

He turned to face her. His troubled blue eyes watched her carefully. "I'm sorry I'm bothering you with this. If I called in the state police, the reporters would be swarming all over the mountain by now. Our killer would know we found two bodies and make a run for it."

She stared at him. "You think the killer lives on this mountain?"

"Definitely."

"But isn't that stupid? This is a small community. If someone is killing the guests, don't you think someone else would notice?"

"We have a lot of woods, Alex. Secrets are everywhere. I'm working closely with the sheriff so we can keep the state police out. If you see or hear anything, tell me."

She shuddered. "If the killer doesn't come after me, you mean."

He kissed her lightly on the cheek. "Thank you, Alex. I do appreciate your help. Do me one favor and keep your wits about you. Okay?"

"All right." His words made her rotate and look in all directions. "Why?"

"Just do it...please. I need to find out why this happened, and I need some pretty solid proof before I let the mountain people know."

She nodded and started down the path.

Charles called a short time later. She resisted the urge to ignore it. He would only worry.

"I wanted to drive you back," he said.

"I needed to walk." *And breathe. And think.*

"Did you reach the cabin yet?"

"I'm in sight of it now."

"Good. Please be careful, Alex. I don't want anything to happen to you."

Leaving would guarantee that. *Oh, hell.* New York wasn't any safer.

"Henrietta tells me she invited you to the star party tonight. Are you still coming?"

"Oh, sure. I need a bit of cheering up."

"Me, too. This stuff is downright depressing. I'll see you tonight." He ended the connection.

She stared at her phone. Her caretaker again. No warm feeling this time, however. Charles lived on the mountain. The killer lived on the mountain. She prayed to God that he had nothing to do with the murders of these two women.

Chapter Ten

It was a lovely night for a star party, cold but nonetheless lovely. No wind. A sky without a stray cloud. Not even the sliver of a moon. Black as black should be, a phenomenon she struggled with since her arrival. A city as large as Manhattan glowed at all hours. Up here, she was lucky to see a porch light.

Alex drove her orange Yugo onto the elementary school parking lot and eased into an empty slot. Little red lanterns dotted the open field behind the school. A path of sorts leading into the darkness. Small groups of people milled about, both adults and children. Some kids ran around as if they overdosed on caffeine. A few elderly adults sat in lawn chairs with blankets over their knees sipping steamy cups of hot fluid. Barbara was one of them. Alex waved. The popular spot was Henrietta's refreshment table. A crowd had gathered around it, chitchatting over cups of coffee. Almost all of them watched her approach.

A stranger in their midst.

Lucy ran full-tilt across the field as Alex reached the table. Alex caught her up in her arms. They hugged. "No Elmo tonight?" The little girl shook her head and gave Alex a kiss.

"Alexandra, welcome!" Henrietta announced. "Everybody, this is Dr. Alexandra Colter from New York. She's staying in our Rosebay cabin."

Polite greetings followed. A loud chortle caught everyone's attention, and all heads turned. Mrs. O'Reilly hurried as fast as her chubby legs carried her, arms outstretched. Alex quickly lowered Lucy to the ground before Mrs. O'Reilly crushed them both in that large bosom. And not a moment too soon. Seconds later, Michael ran up for his hug.

"How's Bluto?" Alex asked him.

"The vet said you did a good job. I only have to give him an-ti-bi-otics for three days."

"We can't thank you enough," Mrs. O'Reilly said. "Charles told me you might appreciate one of my casseroles as payment."

"I—huh—you don't have to do that."

"Nonsense. I want to. Besides, he told me you can't cook. How about a nice Shepherd's Pie?"

"I love Shepherd's Pie!"

"Good. I'll have Charles bring it around."

Michael shuffled his feet while tugging on his grandmother's jacket. "I got your chair out, Grandma."

She looked down at him. "Did you remember my blanket?"

"Uh-huh. Can I go look at stars now?"

Mrs. O'Reilly rolled her eyes but off they went with a wave. Alex turned back to Henrietta's table as another woman handed her a cup of coffee. "You'll need this, dear. Most of us are freezing our toes off."

Alex loaded her cup with cream and sipped. It was wonderfully hot. "It certainly is dark out here," she commented.

"A necessary evil," one man volunteered. "Charles won't allow any white lights, not even a flashlight. Interferes with night vision, he says. Only red lights which you see scattered every where so we won't trip and break our necks."

"Charles is out in the field," Henrietta said with a nod toward the darkness.

Alex looked down at Lucy. "Shall we go find Charles?"

In answer, Lucy took her hand and pulled. She happily led the way out onto the field where three large telescopes stood on tripods. Two older teenagers handled two of the scopes. They made adjustments and helped the smaller children onto metal crates so they could see into the eyepiece. Charles operated the third scope. He turned as they approached.

"Oh, great, coffee, thanks!" He grabbed Alex's cup and drank half the contents before she could forewarn him. He made a face. "Yuck, cream!"

"You're welcome," she said. So much for a nice cup of coffee. She finished what remained then tossed the cup in the trash bin. "What are we looking at?"

"Jupiter. I have a contest going to see who can find the most moons. You have to be 10 years old and under."

"I guess that leaves me out. Can I look anyway?"

"Of course. Just get in line."

Alex looked down at Lucy. "You qualify for the contest. Want to try?"

When their turn came, Alex helped Lucy onto the crate. Charles made adjustments to focus the target, and they both encouraged Lucy to find the moons.

"How many are there?" Alex asked Charles.

He wagged a finger. "That's cheating. Everyone has to put the moons on paper as to their position around Jupiter along with the time they observed. How many do you see, Lucy?"

She held up three fingers.

"Look harder," Alex encouraged. "Then go draw them on a piece of paper."

She giggled happily before jumping from the crate. She ran toward a table covered with paper and pencils where other kids busily etched their drawings. An old codger sat nearby giving them times.

"My turn," Alex said but stopped when she met his gaze. He stared with wide-eyed amazement. "What?"

"She giggled!"

"Yes, it's the second time I've heard it. I think she's about to break out of that shell." She looked into the eyepiece, saw a sky sparkling with stars, but had no idea if a planet was among them. She glanced up at Charles who still stared. "What's wrong?"

He hesitated for several long seconds. Then he leaned close. "I like your earmuffs."

"That's not what you were going to say." No proof. Just a feeling. Like when a patient downplays the severity of their pain. "I took a quick trip to the valley this afternoon to buy some warmer clothes. Do they look dumb?"

"I think you look very nice. I'm glad you came."

"I promised Lucy."

"And you never break a promise. I remember."

Their moment alone was just that—a moment. Children of all ages surrounded them, urging Charles to judge their papers. "No, no, that's Miss Warner's job. There she is, over there."

The whole group ran to this tall...redhead. A flaming redhead, like a dragon in the glow of the red lanterns. The children jumped and waved their papers at her, but her eyes were riveted to Alexandra.

Oh, joy.

"Miss Warner is one of our school teachers," Charles explained. "The kids love her."

Double joy.

"She's very attractive."

"Maybe, but you, my dear, are the most stunning woman I have ever seen." He put his face close. *"That's* what I was going to say earlier."

Her face flushed.

"I didn't mean to embarrass you," he whispered.

"You surprised me, Charles. I never expected a comment so personal from a man who doesn't smile. I'm not even sure you have teeth in that mouth of yours." She looked into the eyepiece. "Which one is Jupiter?"

"I need to reposition the scope. The Earth is in constant motion. The higher the power of the scope, the faster the object appears to move. There are computerized motors available that will keep the scope on an object, but I like hunting on my own. It's more fun." He looked into the eyepiece while turning two knobs until he was satisfied. He motioned for her to look.

Jupiter at high power! A phenomenal sight! A big, bright round globe. And she distinctly saw six moons! "Wow, this is great!"

"All right, you two. No private lessons."

The comment came from the tall redhead. She swaggered toward them on long legs that were poured into tight blue jeans. She also flashed Alex a glare that would freeze a hot sun. She slipped her arm through Charles'. The maneuver was a possessive one.

"Sharon Warner," he said, "meet Dr. Alexandra Colter, our Rosebay guest." He slipped his arm out of hers to help a little boy onto the crate.

"Nice to meet you, doctor."

Yeah, Alex really believed that.

The woman was incredibly tall, close to six feet. It wouldn't be difficult for her to squash her competition like a bug. Being civil, Alex took the outstretched hand and immediately felt the crushing grip. A cruel curl lifted one corner of her coral-colored lips as a pair of green eyes danced.

"You drive like a maniac," Alex said when Sharon dropped her hand.

"Oh, it's this mountain road, so treacherous at times. Don't you agree, Charles?"

"Uh-huh."

The man was oblivious. He was busy helping the little boy with the telescope.

"You really shouldn't bother him, doctor. He's so busy with the children on nights like this. He has very little time to entertain our guests."

The defiant badger rose from the bottom of her spine. That same badger helped her face the bully in the neighborhood schoolyard when no one else stood by her side. Even now. She stood alone facing the tall redhead because Charles was too busy with the little boy. Alex wanted to pull out the flaming red hair one strand at a time, maybe rip out both green eyeballs with it and use them as soccer balls.

Lucy ran over and grabbed Alex by the hand. She tugged. A welcomed interruption. *The girl must be psychic.* "Yes, my little one, what is it?"

Lucy dragged her away from Charles and Sharon

across the field directly to James. He stood alone sipping coffee.

"Hi," he said cheerfully. "I thought you might need a little rescuing so I sent in the troops."

Alex laughed, gave Lucy a big kiss and watched her run toward the refreshment table.

"Don't I get a kiss? I gave the command."

"Lucy did all the work, but thank you, James. I did need to get away from her." He wore a flannel shirt and blue jeans, but she asked anyway. "Are you on duty?"

"Truthfully, Doc, I'm always on duty. Being the only cop around has its disadvantages."

"I noticed you don't carry a radio."

"That's because it takes two people for a radio to work. Otherwise, it sits in the trunk. There is no police station either. I work out of my home. People around here call my cell if they need me. It should be posted on your refrigerator, and you should have it in your cell by now."

She laughed. "Yes, it's in my cell now. What if you need help? Who do you call?"

He sipped his coffee. "Charles is my first call. Second call goes to Harry at the garage. Usually the three of us can handle a situation. Harry may be small, but he packs a good punch." He studied her over the steaming cup. "What's your opinion of Sharon?"

"Other than the fact that she is a lousy driver?" She grunted while scanning the crowd. "I have no opinion."

"Sure you do. I saw it in your face."

"You saw a badger."

He jerked. "A what?"

"Never mind. She's—huh—attractive."

"I didn't ask how she looked."

"You asked for an opinion."

He peered at her knowingly.

"All right, all right, she just tried to crush my surgical hand. She has a very strong grip."

He chuckled. His handsome face finally brightened. "There, see, that wasn't so bad. The truth is she hates every woman who gets near Charles."

"I already got that message. Loud and clear, in fact. I was only looking through the telescope."

"Doesn't matter. You were near him." He tossed his cup in the trash. "The bunch of us are friends, Alex. We grew up together, all of us: Charles, Harry, Sharon, and me. We tend to be protective of each other."

"That's nice." She said it with disgust while stuffing her hands in her coat pockets. She felt the gloves she bought to keep her hands warm. She left them there, too.

James looked at her curiously. "How do you feel about Charles?"

She shrugged. "He's a nice enough guy."

"That's all you can say?"

"Well, if I said any more than that, Sharon might plow her car straight into the cabin. Why?"

"Because I need to take my mind off my job for a while. In the process, I intend to make him insanely jealous." He lifted her chin upward and brought his lips down onto hers. It was a warm kiss with a pleasant taste of coffee. When he pulled away, his blue eyes twinkled. "I never kissed a doctor before."

"I never kissed a cop." They both laughed. "Thanks, James. You made my day."

"I can make your day every day if you want."

A tempting offer. A fling with such a gorgeous

man would be erotic fun, a cap on an unusual vacation.

His cell phone rang. He made a face when he saw the caller ID. "So much for taking my mind off my job. It's the county sheriff." He brushed his hand lightly across her cheek and took the call. She walked away to give him some privacy.

As attractive as James was, Alex felt nothing from his kiss or even the touch on her cheek. Yet, Charles merely touched her hand, and her insides flipped. Clearly, Charles affected her. It felt nice. It also surprised her to realize such a startling revelation.

Lucy ran to her side. The little psychic again. She grabbed Alex by the hand and tugged. "Where to?" Alex asked.

Lucy led her to a grassy knoll where people and blankets covered the field. Adults and children alike had their eyes glued skyward. Alex glanced up, half expecting to see a flying saucer. Lucy dragged her to Henrietta all stretched out on a blanket, looking comfortable with her hands clasped behind her head.

"Best part of the whole night," she said as they approached. "Care to join us?"

Alex stood staring in awe at the array of people on blankets. "What's going on?"

"There's a meteor shower tonight. It should start any second. Have a seat."

Alex sat on the blanket and crossed her legs. "How often do you do this?"

"Whenever we can, maybe four or five times a year. It's fun for the kids and relaxing for us. I love just lying here and staring at the stars. Charles and Sharon are the busiest because of the telescopes. Now, lay down, Alexandra. You need to stare up at the sky."

She wasn't ready to lie down. She watched Charles and Sharon dismantle the scopes.

"They're good friends," Henrietta said kindly.

Alex looked at her. "You say that like it matters."

"I'm hoping it does."

Alex watched them carry the telescopes toward the parking lot. "Sharon doesn't like me."

"She doesn't like any woman who gets near Charles."

She looked back at Henrietta. "I just had this conversation with James."

"Well, you're having it again. She is actually a very nice girl. Bear in mind that Sharon and Charles grew up together. She might be protective of him."

"He should marry her then."

Henrietta made a face. "I wondered about that. All of us would like to see him get married again." Her head turned sharply. "He told you, I hope."

"Yes, he did."

"Good. He's very private. James is just the opposite. That kiss he gave you, for example, out in the open for the world to see."

"I doubt he achieved his objective."

Henrietta's eyebrows shot up. "Which was?"

"He said he wanted to make Charles insanely jealous. I hope those two guys don't sleep together."

Henrietta chuckled softly. "Lay down, Alexandra. You're sticking out like a sore thumb."

Alex obeyed. Lucy immediately wiggled over and snuggled up against her. A strange and powerful emotion swept through her as she positioned Lucy closer to her chest. The emotion was so strong, she actually pulled back just to see if it were only Lucy in her arms. Alex glanced at Henrietta, feeling somewhat awkward at Lucy's maneuver, but Henrietta's brown eyes shifted from Lucy to Alex then back again until a warm smile spread onto her lips.

"Everything all right?" Henrietta asked casually.

Alex nodded stupidly. For the first time in her life, everything felt right. This little girl. The mountain. The people.

And she hadn't a clue what to do about it.

Chapter Eleven

Two beauties on a blanket. A brunette holding a little blonde. A woman with a child in her arms. The way it should be. What eluded him for years. Those were his thoughts as he watched them sleep. A powerful sense of wonder flowed through Charles as he listened to their soft breaths. Alexandra should be curled up in his arms instead of Lucy in hers. His own fault really. So friggin' cautious. She affected him from the moment she set foot on the mountain, yet he put up a shield. Armor more like it. A defensive mechanism after so many disappointments. He always took chances when he was younger. Why not now? Especially with her. She had such expressive eyes. When she focused on him, he felt lost within them. She was honest and open and real. Because of that, he needed to seriously reevaluate his opinion of doctors. He always found them to be so remote, like this mountain, like himself. Remote and untouchable. She changed everything. Even Lucy. Charles smiled to himself because Lucy wore Alexandra's earmuffs. They looked cute on her, too.

"We pretty much waited till the last minute," Henrietta whispered as she came alongside. She stared down at them. "They look so peaceful."

Indeed. The star party ended an hour ago. Everyone packed up and left while carrying sleeping children in their arms. Only two vehicles remained in the parking lot: the orange Yugo and the Red Baron. By some miracle, he was able to get rid of Sharon.

"Do you want to wake Alexandra, or should I?" Henrietta asked.

"I'll do it." It was a chance to feel the hair that looked so silky. He wanted to feel it the day he took the pine needles out of her hair. She was too tempting and too close in the truck cab for him to take the liberty. He squatted and touched. Yes, it was silky. He let it run through his fingers. How he longed to hold her. From the first day they met, he wanted her in his arms. Not just a simple caress. The whole woman. To feel every soft curve. To taste her lips. To smell her scent. She felt something for him. Every fiber in him told him so. Did she know it? Was she waiting for him to make the first move?

"It might be a good idea to call her name," Henrietta suggested.

He really didn't want to wake her, but they would freeze out here if he didn't do something. He touched the hair again. "Alexandra."

She jerked awake. Sleepy eyes stared up, blinking the sleep away. He immediately felt the longing to taste those soft lips, to prove if they were as soft as he imagined. Then her gaze shifted to Henrietta then down at Lucy cuddled in her arms. Charles put a finger to his lips as he reached to pick up the little girl. He preferred Alexandra in his arms, but he had only himself to blame for the delay. The beautiful doctor affected everyone she met in her short time on the mountain. She affected him the most and, without question, the fastest. She put love back into his heart. He'd thought it disappeared forever.

"Oh, God, I'm frozen!" Alex said while keeping her voice low. She rubbed her legs to get some circulation going.

Henrietta helped her to her feet then grabbed the blanket and gave it a good shake. "Come on, dear."

"What time is it?"

"A little after midnight. We didn't have the heart to wake you two so we waited until everything was cleaned up."

"I missed the meteor shower." She yawned.

"Next time, dear. Here, fold this blanket for me." She hurried to get ahead of Charles so she could open the truck door and hop in. Charles placed Lucy on her lap and quietly closed the door. Alexandra handed him the blanket that she haphazardly folded. He threw it in the bed of the truck, not giving a damn whether it was folded or not.

"Are you awake enough to drive?" he asked.

"Oh, sure." She yawned again. "I can't believe how well I sleep up here. I wasn't even tired when I hit the blanket." Another yawn. "Thanks for an interesting evening. I'm sorry I missed everything." She shook herself and started toward her car. Charles walked right along with her. "I'll be all right," she said.

"I know you will, but I'm walking you to your car anyway." He opened the car door. The metal felt light, too thin. A good wind should blow the tin can right off the mountain. She deserved to drive something more substantial. "I could easily drive you back to the cabin."

"No, I'll be okay...really."

He waited for her to start up and drive away before walking back to the pickup truck. He experienced a profound sense of loss for some reason. Her driving away without him had to be the cause.

****

Charles carried Lucy as Henrietta rushed ahead to open doors and turn on some lights. They reached Lucy's bedroom when the little girl stirred. Her head lifted while sleepy eyes looked around. She blinked up at Charles. "Where's Alex?" she asked.

A cry escaped from Henrietta's throat. She slapped a hand over her mouth to stifle it. Even Charles stopped in his tracks to stare at the little blonde in his arms.

"I want Alex," Lucy said sleepily. She rubbed her eyes.

"Alex has gone to bed," Charles said, visible shaken. "You can see her tomorrow."

"I like Alex."

"Me, too." He said it with some irony.

"She gave me her earmuffs."

"They look very nice on you."

Tears flowed freely from Henrietta's eyes as she pulled down the blankets on Lucy's bed. She and Charles worked carefully to remove the little girl's jacket and boots without waking her further. "What about the earmuffs?" Charles whispered.

"Leave them. She'll take them off when she's ready."

"I want to kiss Alex good night," Lucy murmured.

"You can kiss me, and I will give it to her," Charles said gently.

Lucy kissed him on the cheek and promptly fell back to sleep.

All this time, the girl never spoke, never a cry, never a sound. They tried everything to coax the voice.

Nothing worked. Why now all of a sudden? What magical power did this woman possess that others lacked?

"Didn't I tell you that woman was special?" Henrietta said barely controlling her voice. "I knew it, Charles. I felt it the moment we met. You will give her a kiss from me, too." She kissed his other cheek. "Now you have two reasons to kiss her. If you let that woman leave this mountain, I swear I will sell the store and move to an old folk's home in Roanoke." She fussed with Lucy's sheets. "Wait for me in the living room."

He had to wait. His knees were so wobbly, he knew he couldn't make it back to his truck. He flopped onto a recliner.

Henrietta came charging out like a bull. She pointed her finger at him in anger. "You need to break out of this armor you put yourself in, Charles. You've kept your feelings clammed up too long. Every woman you've dated since your divorce has abruptly called it off. I don't know what the hell you're doing with them, but it has to stop."

"I'm cursed, Henrietta. I don't want anything to happen to her."

She pulled back, startled. "What are you talking about? Who in the world put that idea in your head? Your father? Is that why you closed your heart?" She took a deep breath since her voice rose in octave, enough to wake half the mountain. She tried again with more vocal control. "Your father is dead, Charles, long buried alongside your mother."

"No, it isn't my father," he said irritably. He jumped to his feet and paced.

How could he tell her? No one must know what

happened to his other women. The secret gnawed at his heart, and there wasn't a pill on this earth to help it.

"Everyone on the mountain sees how you feel," she continued. "It was only the second day when we saw the change in your face, in your step. Everyone sees it, Charles, everyone except Alexandra. The poor woman doesn't have a clue how you feel."

"She might prefer James. I should break his neck for kissing her."

"Why? Because he beat you to it? I'm surprised you even noticed. You and Sharon had your heads huddled together far more than usual."

That brought out another bout of pacing. "That was Sharon's doing. She kept talking so low I couldn't hear her. I was pissed as hell when she interrupted Alex and me. Then the next thing I know, I've got all the kids at my scope because Sharon told my helpers to disassemble theirs. She never did that before. So, yeah, I noticed Alex and James." He hit a fist into his open palm. "I should rearrange his nose."

"No, you don't want to hurt James. He's your best friend, and he kissed her on purpose to get you riled up. He wants you to do something before it's too late."

Charles looked at her sharply. "He told you that?"

"Hell, no! Alexandra said he kissed her to make you insanely jealous. She had no clue what he meant."

"Well, it worked. I'm jealous."

"The kiss meant nothing to her."

He eyed her carefully. "You don't know that."

"Actually, I do. A woman does not kiss a man while keeping her hands in her pockets."

Surprise covered his face. The pacing stopped. "What's that supposed to mean?"

"It means, dear, that when a woman likes the kiss given her, her hand will reach up to touch the face that gave her that kiss. Trust me on this."

"You're making it up."

"No, I'm not. It's practically inbred. If her arm goes around your neck while you're kissing her, then she wants more of you. Try it on Alexandra and see what she does. I'm almost convinced she won't keep her hands tucked away like she did with James."

"She was probably cold."

Henrietta shook her head in disbelief. "You're as dense as she is. Look, Charles—" She grabbed his hand and held it. "Don't try to analyze this. You had one bad marriage. That doesn't mean you'll have another. You were young at the time and trying to appease your father. Everyone on this mountain wants to see you fall in love again. Let your heart guide you before it's too late."

Alexandra's time on the mountain was short. She scheduled herself for a week, and the week slowly crept to an end. If he didn't get his ass moving, all would be lost.

It was time to take another chance.

Chapter Twelve

Alexandra slipped out of the Yugo and stretched. She felt wide awake and refreshed after her nap. She entered the cabin, threw on some lights, and tossed a few logs into the stove. She still felt frozen. Her ass, her legs, her toes. Every inch of her needed the warmth of a fire, but she wasn't ready to call it a night. A meteor shower filled the sky. What little she knew about them, they do not start *any second now* as Henrietta stated nor do they stop like throwing a switch. There had to be residual strays shooting around, and she wanted to see them. She grabbed a blanket and flashlight and hurried outside.

It would be nice to enjoy the night with someone. She doubted any of her colleagues had the interest. They primarily partied to relax. She rarely joined them, preferring instead to go home and put her feet up. Here though, this mountain, these people made her think differently. In so short a time, she developed a sense of belonging, a sense of community.

Maybe it was time to get the hell off the mountain.

Headlights coming up the drive stopped her. She recognized the roar of the engine, but he drove at a normal speed. After his last two unexpected visits, she cringed at the prospect of this next one. She remained on the porch as the Red Baron parked alongside the Yugo.

"I'm checking to see if you got back okay," Charles said while stepping out, "and no, we didn't find another body."

He read her mind. "Thank God for small favors," she said.

"I do have good news, however. Lucy spoke!"

She smiled. "I knew she would."

He approached the porch. "You don't seem very surprised."

"I'm a doctor, Charles. I knew she had a voice in her. It was only a matter of time when she used it."

He put one boot up onto the porch and leaned against a post. They stood at eye level. They also stood too close. The magnet pulled her again. She had this overpowering urge to lean over and kiss him. She wanted to feel his arms around her; she wanted to taste his lips. She wanted to feel his strength, his power.

She wanted her breath back. She clutched the blanket closer to her chest instead.

She had no right to want this man. It was merely a physical attraction, nothing more, a hormonal urge to be satisfied. She told herself over and over he wasn't interested. Common sense said not to get involved. Alexandra Colter was a visitor with no plans to stay. She belonged in New York. She had enormous bills to pay. She had neither the time nor energy to get involved with anyone especially a man so far away from her home base. So what if the people made her feel welcomed. So what if this man made her hormones do cartwheels. She didn't belong here.

Her heart told another story.

"I just left a very happy Henrietta who was bawling her eyes out," he said.

"What did Lucy say?" she asked, thankful for the casual air.

"She asked for you."

Her eyebrows shot up. "She did?"

"Don't act so surprised. That little girl loves you."

Alex smiled because she had a strange feeling she loved her, too. The little girl activated a maternal instinct she never knew she had. "You didn't have to drive all the way up here. You could have called."

"Your cabin is on my way home. Besides, I wanted to ask you something."

"I'm listening."

His eyes scanned her from head to toe. It was a calculated scan, one filled with doubt. He clearly debated his question. "Why did you kiss James tonight?"

That surprised her. She stepped back. "I didn't. He kissed me."

"You didn't stop him either."

"It wasn't necessary. I enjoyed it."

His whole face changed into a storm cloud. His gaze grew shuttered and guarded, his lips tight, jaw set. Was James right? Did it make him jealous? The big question, why should it matter? "What's bothering you, Charles?"

The cloud rumbled. The light from the cabin windows glowed on his face, and she distinctly saw anger. "Did James break some unwritten rule? The no natives fraternizing with the guests rule?" No answer. His gaze continued to scan, study, analyze, dissect. "You're not answering my question." She had a lot of practice with male patients who stubbornly refused to answer simple questions. An ego thing, she knew.

"Talk to me, Charles."

He made a face. "James isn't breaking any rules," he grumbled. "I am."

She started. "What are you talking about?"

Again, no answer. He watched her with growing uncertainty. Then suddenly, he asked, "Why the blanket and flashlight?"

She looked at them since she forgot what she held in her arms. "I thought I'd sit on the bench and see what was left of the meteor shower."

His lips spread into a half-cocked grin. "There's no meteor shower tonight. I say it to get the kids calmed down. They're usually all keyed up at these events so everyone gets on a blanket and stares up at the sky. Most of the kids fall asleep, like you and Lucy."

"Oh, phoo! I thought I finally had a chance to see a meteor shower. You can't see one in Manhattan unless the meteor falls on your head." She kicked a leaf off the porch, unable to hide her disappointment. Then she looked at him hopefully. "Anything coming up?"

He shook his head. "You'll always see a stray meteor in a dark sky. The conditions tonight are perfect. If you'd like, we could sit out for a while, that is if you want some company."

Company. Someone to watch the sky with. Still, with him? Too damn tempting. Her brain dismissed her feelings for him as irrelevant, but her heart felt the loneliness lift every time he came near. Despite the conflict, she heard herself say, "That's a nice idea, Charles." *Playing with fire, no doubt about it.*

The black cloud lifted. He took the blanket but left her carrying the flashlight, which she willingly used. They walked out to the bench. When they got there,

Charles opened the blanket and wrapped it around her shoulders. She noticed he wore no jacket, only a flannel shirt. "What about you?" She indicated the blanket.

"I wouldn't mind sharing."

She went to remove the blanket, but he grabbed hold of it with both hands and stopped her. With a firm grip at her collar, he closed the distance between them. Her breath caught at the intensity in his gaze. Was he about to do what she wanted him to do, what drifted into her mind since the day she arrived? She looked up at him in question.

"Lucy said a few more words that I need to pass on," he began. "She wanted to kiss you good night. I told her to kiss me, and I would pass it along." He took hold of her chin and turned her head. He kissed her left cheek, an impersonal kiss, quick and light. "This next one is from Henrietta because you made her so happy." He turned her head to the opposite side and kissed her right cheek, again quick and light.

She smiled up at him. "Tell them thank you."

"I'm not finished. This next one is from me." He released the blanket and wrapped his thick arms around her, pressing her close against his chest. He tilted her chin upward and waited for her protest. When none came, his lips met hers. His lips were soft and warm like she imagined. He nibbled, he teased until a kiss came packed with power and heat. He captured her mouth in a way no man had ever done. His lips revealed hunger, an insatiable hunger demanding a response, which she surprisingly gave him. Her lips parted to take him in, but she wanted more. She slipped her hands into his hair to hold his head close only to hear a faint cry escape from his throat. He crushed her against him.

Gad, he tasted good, he smelled wonderful, and her body screamed for his, but it wasn't right. She was falling for this damn man, and she shouldn't. Unable to bring herself to push him away, she let him sap what little resistance remained. Her bones turned to mush.

He caught her. "Are you all right?"

"Wow!"

"Yeah, wow. I haven't kissed a woman like this in a long time."

"I've got news for you, mister. No man ever kissed me like that. You kissed me like you meant it."

"I did mean it." As if to prove it, he kissed her again. Their tongues danced.

"We could go into the cabin," she whispered.

His face changed as he pulled back. The warmth disappeared to be replaced by...panic?

She needed to get her vision checked.

"That wouldn't be wise," he said.

She broke free. "Are you kidding me?" She died and went to hell. Anger sprang to the surface. "I know arousal when I see it, Charles."

"Not yet, Alexandra."

She stepped back, shocked. "Not yet? What the hell does that mean?" Was this man for real? "Since when is it so difficult to get a guy to drop his pants?" She blurted the words and regretted it. For some reason, she felt like a cheap whore, and the thought of it devastated her. She put all her fingers into her hair and scratched. *Better her hair than his gorgeous eyes.* "Sorry. I'm on edge thanks to you."

He said nothing. He merely picked up the blanket and gave it a good shake. He wrapped it around his shoulders, sat on the bench, and held the blanket open.

119

"You still want to see meteors?"

"How can you be so nonchalant? Don't you realize what you just did to me?"

"Yes, I realize because it did the same to me. I won't have a fling with you, Alexandra. You deserve better. Now, do you want to see meteors or not?"

She did. Besides, fling or nay, she refused to be tormented in hell alone. His erection strained against his blue jeans, and she intended to keep it that way or be damned in the process. She sat next to him on the bench and fit herself perfectly under his arm. She put her feet up on the seat as he threw the blanket over her.

The heat of his body finally thawed her frozen bones although his kiss did a good job of getting her started. She took his arm and draped it across her chest, realizing with a start that her fingers failed to wrap around his wrist. Moreover, his bicep draped like a brick between her breasts. Nice. Attractive and strong. *Yeah, big deal.* She glanced skyward. "What am I looking for?"

"You can't look in any one spot," he began. "You need to let a flash of light hit your eyes. Most meteors are quick; others have a tail to follow."

They fell silent. She kept her gaze skyward, hoping to catch that flash of light. Unfortunately, her attention wavered because of the comfort this man gave, a comfort she never experienced with any man. She heard his heart beating in his chest, a steady rhythmic pattern that a cardiologist would love. His breath stirred her hair. It blew warm against her scalp. The arm draped across her chest put his hand at her hip, and his fingers gave a slow caress on her butt.

Not yet, he said. No man ever said those two words

to her before. When then? "Why did you kiss me, Charles?"

"Because I couldn't go any longer."

Neither could she when she thought about it. "Yet, you don't want to follow through. Care to explain?"

He kissed her hair. "No."

He was hiding something. She felt it. Sharon perhaps? Or someone else waiting in his bed? She knew so little about him. She decided to let it rest by changing the subject. "Did you know those two dead women, Charles?"

His arm tightened against her chest. The fingers on her butt froze. "Yes."

"James said there were no locals missing. Were they guests?"

"No, Alexandra, they were not guests. Both those women lived in the valley."

She rubbed his arm lightly until it relaxed. His fingers again caressed her hip.

"Would someone come looking for you if you never showed up?" he asked.

What a strange question! She turned to look at him. "Friends and colleagues more likely. Why?"

He eased her back under his arm. "Those two women never had anyone come around to ask questions. It's as if no one cared. It irks me to realize this. Being alone doesn't mean being forgotten. Everyone should have someone who cares."

It surprised her to hear him say it with such conviction. The subject obviously touched him deeply. "What about you, Charles? Are you alone? Will someone care if you disappeared?"

His arm tightened against her breast again. "No one

is ever alone on this mountain, Alex. Remember that."

She believed it, too. She already felt a part of the mountain, of the people. Why, she wondered, when she hardly knew them? The implication of his statement sunk in, however. She looked up. "The killer knew this," she said.

He shook his head. "I doubt it."

"James said there should be a third victim. Do you believe that?"

"I'm hoping he's wrong, but the pattern is there. This is a black mark on the mountain."

"Yeah, too bad for the victims, too."

He sighed heavily. "I didn't mean to sound callus. Their murders weigh heavily on my mind. It pains me to think we might have a serial killer up here. That constant thought along with the identities of the two women and then you coming here—" Another heavy sigh. "I've been on an emotional rollercoaster."

"Me!" She sat up to face him. "Why me?"

In answer, he lifted her onto his lap. His dark eyes blazed like two burning pieces of coal, and his erection pressed like a steel rod against her hip. She effectively kept him in hell with her. That pleased her to no end.

She moved first. She met his lips with a fierceness that surprised even her. She wanted him. She wanted all of him. The wicked imp in her wanted him in that king size bed tonight.

His cell phone rang. "Go away," he mumbled into her mouth. He sucked half the air out of her lungs before he pulled away in resignation. "I'm still the caretaker," he said sadly and took out his phone. The small screen illuminated the entire bench. She also saw something that caught her eye but let him answer his call first. She rested her head on his shoulder to sniff his aftershave.

"Bad timing," he grumbled into the phone. He listened. His body tensed. "Yes." His voice grew very serious. She lifted her head and met a pair of alert eyes. "All right. Yes, that sounds like a good plan. Very shortly, yes. Where? Good, I'll be there. Be careful, will you?"

The conversation ended. He stared at the phone, his face thoughtful. Alex stopped him from putting the phone away, however. She took it from him and activated the screen.

Her eyes did not deceive her. His screen wallpaper was a photo of her asleep on the hammock. She looked at him blankly.

"I never saw anything more beautiful in my life," he said. "I went home and put it on my computer, too. I hope you don't mind."

She shook her head, too stupefied to answer. She returned the phone.

"Alex—" He struggled to find words. "I—"

"You have to leave," she finished. She was destined to remain in hell...alone.

She looked at him. He looked at her. Their lips pressed together simultaneously, both greedy for more. When they finally separated, his finger traced along her jaw line.

"Yes, I need to leave. It's important. Let me walk you back to the cabin."

"Thanks, but I'll stay out a little while longer."

"No, you won't. You're going back to the cabin."

An authoritative tone. Her eyebrows shot up. "Why?"

"Because I need to know that you are locked in and safe before I leave."

He helped her to her feet and handed her the blanket. He kept the flashlight this time. He used the beam everywhere, up the trees, down the drive, the path.

"What's going on, Charles?"

He didn't answer. Once inside the cabin, he searched the place. The closet, the bathroom. She expected him to flip the mattress to check under the platform. He came back. "I'm going to lock you in using my key. You are not to open the door unless you see me. Is that clear?"

She nodded stupidly, too surprised to form words.

He literally lifted her off her feet and pinned her to the wall. He kissed hard, skillfully separating her lips to thrust his tongue in deep. *Oh, God*! She wanted him so bad. When their lips separated, she met his eyes to see them with a fury that probably matched her own.

He released her and left. She heard the bolt lock. Then the truck started with a roar and squealed away.

Her knees wobbled. Unable to fight it, Alex slid straight down the wall and hit the floor with a thud.

Damn, that man was a great kisser!

Chapter Thirteen

It took a good five minutes before Alex could wobble onto her feet. Her insides jumped like grasshoppers. Even her brain turned into an empty void unable to analyze, diagnosis, or comprehend what happened. Another new first. Bad enough the searing heat remained on her lips. It left her confused and bewildered. She touched them just to reassure herself that they were not on fire.

So who called, and why did he run off so fast? He waved that flashlight beam around as if he searched for someone or something. Who? What? A resident gone amok? An animal chewing and gnawing on a dead...body?

Now that was a definite possibility.

With a heavy sigh, she threw a log into the stove, turned off the lights, and fell into bed. Fully dressed. In no mood to undress when she was so thoroughly turned on.

She awoke to daylight. A glance at the clock on the night table showed the time just after eleven in the morning. She rolled out of bed, stretched, and was about to undress and jump into the shower when she heard the roar of the Red Baron coming up the drive. His speed was excessive. Remembering Charles' command, she peeked out the window to see him behind the wheel then opened the door as the truck skidded to a stop, creating a cloud of dust that promptly whirled and landed on the Yugo.

Charles jumped out, glanced in her direction, but ran around to the passenger side.

She recognized the wild-eyed stare in his eyes. It was one of panic and fear. The same look covered faces of family members rushing a loved one to the hospital. It was an end-of-the-world look, a please-hurry-or-they-will-die look. She automatically switched to her most serious physician face. In their eyes, doctors never worked fast enough. Nurses were flippant and ineffective. X-ray technicians zapped their loved ones with too many gamma rays, and, of course, the bloodsuckers from the lab took all their remaining blood. Most of the time, the injuries weren't serious at all. To them, it was devastating. A loved one was hurt. They wanted them fixed. Action, action, every fiber screamed for action. That was Charles' face as he rounded the truck. He threw open the passenger door, and James rolled out, his arm wrapped in a blood-soaked towel. Charles hurried him toward the cabin. "We need you, doctor."

"So I see. Come on in."

James flopped onto a kitchen chair. He was pale and clearly hurting, but he still flashed a brilliant smile. Alex unwrapped the towel. It was a grease rag!

Men!

Muscle popped through a large gash on his left forearm. She already knew what caused it, but she asked anyway. "What happened?"

"A guy pulled a knife on me. Caught me completely off guard. The county sheriff called last night with a forewarning that he headed our way. Said he was armed and dangerous. Harry, Charles, and I staked out positions along the road to keep an eye out, but he stayed hidden until I accidentally walked up on him a little while ago. Sneaky devil. I didn't see him until he came at me with the knife. Am I going to lose my arm?"

"Hell, no, but you need an emergency room."

"Seventy miles one way, Doc. That's the nearest clinic. I could bleed to death."

She made a face. "You're not bleeding now, James. It just looks awful."

"Then you can stitch me up."

She studied the wound. A clean cut. And deep. "I have some surgical supplies with me, but not enough antiseptic for this size wound."

"Come on. I don't feel like taking a long ride. Just give me a couple of Band-aids to hold it together."

She bit her lip, brows together in a frown, deep in thought. "Tell me, James, what would you do if I wasn't here?"

He gave her a sheepish grin. "I'd have to go to the clinic. But you're not going to send me away, are you, Doc?"

She debated. Seventy miles one way was a deterrent. "All right, suturing a straight cut like this is a lot easier than a jagged one. I'll stitch it." She opened the kitchen cabinet and took out her medical bag.

"You keep it in there?" Charles asked with surprise.

"Yes, along with my purse. Out of sight, out of mind routine. Should I suddenly drop dead, make sure you check all the cabinets before renting the place." She handed him her car keys. "In my car by the spare is a first aid kit. Bring that in for me. I can't remember what I put in it."

Alex retrieved some fresh towels from the bathroom and spread them out on the table in front of James. Charles ran back with the kit. She opened it to see what was inside.

"Sterile water, great!" She said it mostly to herself. And more Betadine! That made her feel better. She took out scissors to cut James' shirtsleeve. "Too bad you weren't wearing a jacket. The knife had very little resistance with just your sleeve."

"Not cold enough for a jacket," he said.

Coulda fooled her.

"Come over here by the sink, James. I'll clean your arm." Afterwards, he returned to the table while she stayed to wash her hands. As she slipped on her one and only pair of surgical gloves, she noticed that every knuckle on his right hand was bruised a deep purple. "What happened to your hand?"

He inspected it with a face glowing with pride. "After the guy sliced me, I beat him to a pulp with my free hand."

"You're packing a gun, James. Why didn't you use it?"

He grinned broadly. "I got more pleasure bashing his face in—which reminds me. Charles, call the county sheriff and tell him we got the guy. A confirmed ID." Then back to her. "One of our locals saw him attack me and called Charles. We handcuffed him to a tree. Charles called Harry to watch him."

Charles went outside to use his phone while she set to work. A few minutes later, he returned. "Sheriff's been notified," he said. "They think the guy's responsible for six assaults. I told them to call before starting up the mountain."

"Then I'm glad I bashed his face in."

Alex glanced up at James. "I don't have enough supplies to stitch up this other guy. I hope you realize that."

"Frankly, I don't care if he bleeds to death. The sheriff can handle him—ouch!"

"Bite a bullet, copper. I have no anesthetic. Be thankful I'm working with sterile supplies."

"I'm grateful, Doc. Trust me, I'm grateful—ouch!"

"Charles—" She glanced up to see him looking slightly green. "Would you please do two things for me? I'm freezing."

He went to the stove and threw in several logs. "What's the second thing?"

"Please make me some coffee."

James bent his head down to force her to make eye contact. His blue eyes sparkled. "Yeah, no offense, Doc, but you look like you just woke up."

"I did, about five minutes before you arrived."

"You slept like that?"

"Yes, I slept like this. I can't tell you how many times I fell into bed fully dressed because of an exhausting schedule."

"You can't use that excuse down here," he said. Then he looked from Charles to Alex and back again. "You know, Charles, I would have bet money that you were with her last night."

"You would have won."

James gave Alex a rueful grin. "I hope I'm not jumping to conclusions here."

"You are. Your call interrupted us."

"Aw, shucks. I'm really sorry about that—ouch!"

She finished the last stitch and double-checked her work. Satisfied, she wrapped his arm with gauze. "If you want to brag about this to your friends, you have 22 stitches in your arm." She threw her gloves in the trash. Because it was a habit, she checked his pulse and took a good look at his face and eyes. It struck her how familiar his eyes seemed, a distinctive deep blue with tiny speckles of gold. She took his bruised hand and pressed.

"Eeouch!" he cried. "Careful."

"I think you broke something. You should get it X-rayed."

"Got a machine in your bag?"

She frowned. "Wise ass." She gathered all the trash and tossed it in the bin. Charles took the soiled towels and the trash bag and placed them in the truck. She washed her hands at the sink. "I need to get you on an antibiotic. Is there a pharmacy up here or do you have to take a train to one?"

"Now who's the wise ass," he said with a grin. "Henrietta is our registered pharmacist. I can take a prescription to her."

Alex wiped her hands. "I don't recall seeing any drugs."

"It's a small closet, always locked. If she doesn't have it, she gets it express shipped. Without a doctor on the mountain, she's not very busy. Renewals, that's all."

"Okay." She wrote the script. "I'll keep it simple with the hope that she has it in stock. You're to take all of it, do you hear me?"

"Yes, ma'am." He placed the script in his breast

pocket.

"If you have pain, take Tylenol."

Charles handed Alex a cup of coffee loaded with cream. She gratefully swallowed half of it, not giving a damn what it did to her esophageal lining. Charles then slipped his hand into her hair and tilted her head upward. They kissed.

"Any final instructions before I cut out of here?" James asked as he stood to his feet.

"I want to see you tomorrow," she said, "Late afternoon will be okay."

"Right." He glanced at both of them and grinned. "I'll wait in the truck."

Charles took her coffee cup and placed it on the table. His arms slipped around her and pulled her close. She melted against him before his lips reached hers. She tried to hold onto some semblance of control, but it proved a wasted effort. She opened her mouth to let his tongue slip in.

It was last night all over again. She wanted this man, and she wanted all of him. But it still wasn't right. She pulled away from his mouth and put her head on his chest. "I don't understand what's come over me," she said.

"When you figure it out, I hope you tell me."

Alex looked up at him with puzzlement. The intensity in his gaze took her aback. It was more than lust, more than greed, hell, she wasn't sure what she saw. "At least I understand why you left so suddenly last night."

"I'm glad the call interrupted us, Alexandra. We're still strangers. I don't want us to rush into something we might regret."

"Sex, you mean."

"Yes, sex. There should be some depth of feeling before that stage."

She stared at him. "Are you talking about love?"

Someone transported her to an alternate universe; she was certain of it. What the hell kind of noble character did she run into? "Why did you start something you knew we would never finish?" she asked with amazement.

"Are we finished?"

Dear Lord! Talk about confused and bewildered! If he kept this up, she'd be strapped in leathers. She broke away from his arms and grabbed her coffee cup. "Yes, we're finished...I guess. I don't know. You're not making any sense."

He shrugged. "I'm through the fulfilling a physical need shit. The next woman I take to bed will be my wife."

Wow. That effectively eliminated her. From a man who resembled an Adonis no less. She gulped the last of her coffee. "At least your intentions are clear." Too clear, and she was not in the mood to admire his nobility. She turned away. "Better not keep James waiting." She said it tartly hoping he would take the hint and get the hell out.

He hesitated, realized the dismissal was final, and nodded as he left the cabin.

Chapter Fourteen

Alexandra took her time after the two men left. She showered, ate a light brunch, and drank a second cup of coffee. Her thoughts constantly drifted to Charles. She fought like mad to keep him out, but there were hardly any distractions. When she poured cream into her coffee, she thought of him drinking it black. When she went out to the bench with her cup, she thought of him sneaking up behind her. She enjoyed everything about the man last night, all wonderful and overwhelming. His lips filled her with an emotion new and puzzling. His arms left her feeling secure and protected. She desperately wanted to feel both again. Most of all, she wanted to understand what the hell it was.

But the man wanted love. Like she had all the time in the world to fall in love. Granted, she developed a passion for him, a strong passion that she failed to understand, but it couldn't possibly be love. She just met him. People don't fall in love that fast. It only happened in a fairy tale, and she gave up on that a long time ago.

A hormonal urge. Definitely a hormonal urge. Nothing more.

She sighed heavily and watched the bright orange rays color the valley below. She would miss this bench when she returned to New York, which should be soon. She needed to return. Confusion clouded her brain.

Total incomprehensible confusion.

Damn you, Charles! You have no right to confuse me like this!

"Alex!"

Alex heard the patter of little feet before she heard her name. Finally, a distraction to get her mind off that man. She turned to see Lucy running toward the bench clutching her red Elmo doll. Alex put her cup on the ground because, as expected, Lucy ran straight toward her and jumped onto her lap. They hugged and kissed.

That powerful emotion surfaced again. Maternal without doubt. Lucy reminded her of what she didn't have: a family, a child, someone to call her own. Not in her cards, she guessed. She lived her life alone, and only the people on this mountain forced her to question it. The hardest part could be the day she needed to pack up and leave.

"Did Charles give you my kiss?" Lucy asked.

"He did, and he gave me Henrietta's as well."

"I'm glad. I want you to stay forever. Promise you'll stay. Nobody wants you to leave."

"I can't promise that, Lucy. I live in New York. That's pretty far away."

Her little face scrunched, deep in thought. "You should marry James. Then you can live in his house."

That surprised her. "Why James?"

"Because I like him. He's a poll-lease-man. That's a good job. Besides, I saw him kiss you last night. That means he likes you."

"You sure are full of opinions for someone who just found her voice."

"I didn't lose my voice."

"That's pretty obvious. You had a lot of people

worried." Alex squeezed her and kissed her hair. "Why didn't you speak until now?"

"I was afraid."

Alex caught her breath. That was not the answer she expected. When she thought about it, she wasn't sure what she expected. "What were you afraid of?"

Lucy clammed up. Sadness flooded her blue eyes, deep blue eyes with tiny speckles of gold.

"We're friends, Lucy. Friends share secrets with a vow never to tell anyone else. Like when I told you I got scared of the fog. You didn't tell anyone, did you?"

She shook her head.

"Well, I'm going to squeeze and hug you and not let you go until you share a secret with me." Alex squeezed her playfully. Lucy giggled, and that quickly, she was sad again. Whatever bothered her went deep. Alex held her and waited.

"My daddy didn't like me," she said finally.

Alex said nothing. She held Lucy close, avoiding any eye contact. The girl was finally talking. She didn't want to screw it up now.

"He drove the car over the cliff because he didn't like me. He was mad at Mommy because of me."

Alex's entire colon tied itself into one big knot. "What did he say?"

"He said I wasn't his child. He knew it for a long time. He hated me. It made Mommy cry."

"You are an impossible little girl to hate, Lucy. Look how quickly we became friends."

She let that sink in before continuing. "Mommy tried to stop him, but he called her all kinds of bad names. Then he hit her. She cried." She fell silent. Alex put her chin on the top of Lucy's head and waited.

"Daddy drove the car over the cliff, Alex. On purpose. He wanted to kill all of us because of me." A tear escaped from her eye. It rolled freely down her cheek and dripped onto her jacket. Alex held her tight.

"You survived, Lucy. That tells me you are very special."

She sniffed. "Do you love me, Alex?"

"I love you very much. And so does Henrietta. That's why you still live on this mountain surrounded by people who love you dearly. You must always remember that." *People who will come looking, who care.*

"Promise you won't tell anyone."

"Yes, I promise. I'll keep your secret, and you'll keep mine. Right?"

"Right." She held up her little finger. Alex hooked her finger, and they sealed the pact.

Alex struggled to hold back her own tears. She wanted to erase Lucy's memory and fill her mind with happy thoughts. She wanted to hold onto her forever and never let go, but common sense prevailed. Henrietta should be looking for her soon. In a short while, daylight will disappear. "You need to get back, Lucy. What do you say I race you home?"

Lucy jumped off her lap with a giggle and ran. "Can't catch me! Can't catch me!"

Amazing how quickly children swing out of a mood. Alex wanted to pop a few antidepressants.

"Can't catch me!"

Alex ran after her, making sure the girl stayed ahead. Once they crossed over the bridge and were in sight of the store, Lucy turned. "I won! I won!" She hopped all over the place.

Alex pretended to be breathless since a three quarter mile run hardly broke out a sweat. "Yes, all right, you won—this time. I demand a rematch."

"I have another secret," she said gleefully.

"Oh, you do, do you? Out with it."

"Charles is going to make you an office in his house. He has lots and lots of room."

The news surprised her. "How do you know?"

"I heard him tell Henrietta. He wants you to stay and take care of all of us. I think that's a great idea."

"Well, he hasn't asked me yet so don't jump to conclusions."

"Don't tell him I told ya."

"I won't." They hugged and off she ran toward the cottage.

An office in his house? More likely an office for himself. Expansion plans to ten cabins meant more caretaker duties. Yes, Lucy misunderstood. An office for the caretaker, not the doctor.

Alex strolled back, contemplating Lucy's story about the accident. Was it true? If so, then Lucy's silence clearly resulted in deep guilt. She blamed herself for the accident and the death of her mother. A horrible memory imbedded in a young mind forever, a nightmare to relive over and over. No wonder she refused to speak.

What a dilemma. Alex promised to keep her secret, but as an adult, she had an obligation to report it. Not that it mattered. The murderer was long dead along with his wife, leaving a lovely little girl without family.

Unless what she suspected proved true.

Alex suddenly stopped and took a good look around. Someone was following her; she felt it. She saw no one. Yet, the feeling remained, and again, she rotated to look. She was alone in the forest, alone with shadows and increasing darkness. She shook herself and continued up the path.

Alex reached the cabin clearing just as the sun touched the peaks on the western mountain range. Charles sat on the bench watching it. Alex stood in the clearing, uncertain whether to approach. The man already had her confused. After Lucy's piece of news, she should just go into the cabin and soak her head.

Oh, hell! She swallowed whatever it was she felt and walked toward the bench. Charles held her coffee cup, the contents tossed. He looked up as she approached. His face displayed the rigidness of a statue.

"If you thought I jumped, you should be looking over the side for me," she teased. She sat, not close but not on the edge either. His brows came together in a frown. He stared absently at the sunset. "What is it, Charles?"

He looked at her and hesitated, just like he did at the star party. "You'd make a wonderful mother."

Her mouth fell open. He pulled that comment out of a hat; she was certain of it. Then a light bulb lit. "You overheard Lucy, didn't you?"

"Very perceptive of you." He stared straight ahead. The red glow of the sunset made her see for the first time how dark his eyes really were. She couldn't distinguish the iris from the pupil. "We always suspected it was a murder/suicide," he continued. "A top-notch forensics team investigated and found no other explanation why the car suddenly went over the cliff. The fact that Lucy survived such a plunge was a sheer miracle."

"She's James' daughter, isn't she?" He nodded without as much as a glance in her direction. "How long have you known?"

"Only since the accident. James became a real basket case after we discovered Lucy dangling from her car seat. We didn't know what was wrong until Henrietta pried it out. I couldn't believe I never saw it."

"Don't blame yourself. It's hard to see something when you look at it every day. It's like driving on the same streets. You don't remember the names of the streets because you traveled the same route hundreds of times. You see Lucy. You see James. Like the names of the streets, you never really look. Human nature."

"You saw it."

"I'm an outsider looking in. I saw the similarities. Why doesn't he tell her?"

"He's afraid. We didn't understand why Lucy clammed up other than the obvious trauma. After a few months of silence, we suspected she had a pretty good idea what went on. It turns out we were right. We had her tested by some of the best experts in the country, and they all said the same thing: her voice was fine. Give her time. The same report over and over. Then you come along and within a week, she's talking. Of all things, she tells you what we suspected all along. She confided in a perfect stranger."

The tone of his voice made her slightly uneasy. "You don't have to sound bitter about it."

His eyes searched her face. She sensed the scrutiny, the questions, and hesitation. "You misunderstand. I'm not bitter at all. I'd like to see you stay."

"Oh." She stared down at her sneakers. "I have no

reason to stay." She wasn't sure she could stay even if she *had* a reason. "Will James tell her now?"

He didn't answer. His eyes still searched her face. Then he turned away. "You can ask him yourself when you see him tomorrow."

"All right, I will. A little girl's happiness is at stake. I'm sure she feels all alone after being rejected by the man she thought was her father. Then the jackass tries to kill them because of her. That's a horrible legacy to carry around. If James doesn't want the responsibility, I'd like to take her back to New York with me."

A bolt of lightning shot across the bench. His face was fierce, angry. "Lucy belongs on this mountain!"

She stared, slightly taken-aback at the fierceness. "Will she turn into a pumpkin if she leaves?"

"That's not what I meant. James won't let you take her away. The only reason I carried her to bed last night was because he was busy getting details about our intruder."

"That's hopeful." She stood to her feet.

Charles grabbed hold of her wrist and held firm. "Alex—"

His grip had none of the gentleness of earlier. It revealed determination, even force. She waited for him to speak. And waited. The words never came. "What's on your mind, Charles?"

He released her wrist and frowned. "Too much is on my mind, unfortunately. I want you to stay on the mountain."

She sat down again. "I can't. I have bills to pay. Huge bills."

"I can lend you some money."

She shook her head. "I won't take it. I'm trying to keep my head above water while I pay off my student loan. I'm down to seventy thousand."

"*Seventy thousand*!"

"Now you understand why I nearly burnt myself out. I figure a couple more years of hard work then I'll be able to relax. I'll work a more humane schedule."

"That's too long for me to wait."

Her brows shot up. "I don't expect you to wait. Why would you?"

"You're so friggin' dense." He jumped to his feet. "I do not want you to leave this mountain!"

She stared at him with growing amazement. He looked angry, confused, and definitely disturbed. It was a rare glimpse at a man who kept his emotions under wraps. He started for the woods.

"Where are you going?"

"To get my truck!"

As he disappeared into the forest, it dawned on her that maybe the two dead women were not allowed to leave the mountain either. She shook the thought from her mind and headed back to the cabin.

Chapter Fifteen

The low roar of the Red Baron echoed through the trees as Alex read a magazine on the sofa. A quick glance at the kitchen clock showed the time as a few minutes past ten. A little late for rounds. She already bathed and lounged in her jammies and robe and was in no mood to go climbing a mountainside after another dead body.

God forbid.

The truck door slammed. The tailgate creaked open and dropped with a bang. He made enough noise to wake a bear in hibernation. When the tailgate slammed shut, she expected the start of the engine to follow. Instead, heavy footsteps vibrated the porch boards. A gentle knock sounded on the door.

She laughed. All that noise but he knocked as if afraid to wake her. "Who is it?" Like she didn't know.

"Charles."

What could he want at this hour? Certainly not her. He left angry earlier, and nothing changed since. That meant he wanted "the doctor", but it didn't explain all the noise. She checked the condition of her robe, fluffed up her hair, and went to the door.

An impeccably groomed man stood in the doorway. He wore well-pressed dress slacks with a crisp white shirt open at the collar. He also wore a lightweight jacket of pale gray that accentuated his dark hair and eyes. She couldn't imagine him unloading wood while wearing such nice clothes, but men were men. James climbed up and down a mountain slope in his nicely pressed cop uniform. She expected no differently with Charles.

Charles' gaze scanned her from head to toe. "You're ready for bed!"

"You obviously have not looked at a clock," she said. "It's after ten, Charles. I wasn't expecting company." She scanned him with equal scrutiny. He was breathtaking to say the least. "You look like you just got back from a date."

"No, just starting. I'm about to ask the most beautiful woman on this mountain to go out. I don't dress up often so how do I look?"

"You look very nice." Actually, she had yet to catch her breath. She swallowed hard. "Who's the lucky lady?"

"You. There's a fantastic sky above us."

She stepped back, eyes wide. "I'm your date?"

"If you don't mind this spur-of-the-moment notice. You were short-changed last night."

She wouldn't describe it that way, but she let it pass. "Not tonight, Charles."

"This is your last clear night, Alexandra. The forecast is for partly cloudy skies for the next three nights. You haven't seen any meteors yet, and your time with us is almost over. If you want to see meteors, it must be tonight."

He had a point. Seeing a few meteors would be the highlight of a very unusual vacation. Yet, she didn't want a repeat of last night. She wasn't sure she could handle it. She hesitated.

"I need a chance to apologize, Alexandra."

She wasn't interested in an apology. She was interested in meteors. "All right, let me change." She grabbed some clothes and went into the bathroom. "Coffee is on the counter."

"Maybe later. Wear something warm. It's chilly out."

She rejoined him while finger combing her hair. Charles stood where she left him by the door. He looked nervous and slightly apprehensive. "Why did you dress up?"

"To show I have more in my wardrobe besides blue jeans and flannel shirts. Ready?"

She threw on her jacket, and they stepped out into a very black night.

He was right. A mass of stars twinkled above them. She stopped to stare straight up. "I never knew there were so many stars in the sky," she said with awe. "Will we see a moon tonight?"

"We're in a new moon phase. So no, you won't see a moon. It's best to look at stars without the interference of a bright moon. Watch your step."

His large hand slipped over hers like that day in the fog. The gentleness of it contrasted with his afternoon grip. When he looked back, sparks flew. She refused to let it ignite any feelings. The man caused her to question her own sanity.

They followed a path of little red lanterns up to the bench. It brought back the memory of her walk through the enchanted forest with tiny gnomes hiding behind mushrooms. As they approached the bench, she realized with a start that he had more than little red lanterns set up.

Alex stopped dead.

Off to the side of the bench stood a small round table. A white lace tablecloth covered it. A bottle of wine and two glasses sat on one side, a plate of cheese and crackers on the other, and between them, a large bouquet of red roses. She stood there, too stunned to move.

Charles took her by the shoulders and turned her to face him. He gently caressed her arms. "I often have trouble putting my feelings into words. When you told me today that you had no reason to stay, I knew in my heart that there was no way I could let you go without taking my best shot. I came up with this romantic night under the stars with the hope that you'll fall in love with me. I'm correct, am I not, to say that you are not in love with me?"

She nodded, totally mute.

"I don't want you to leave. *We* don't want you to leave. From the moment you arrived, everything about you felt right, like a magical aura suddenly appeared on the mountain. I can't explain it any better than that. You are beautiful, you are kind, you are authoritative, and you are naïve. That package as a whole is how everyone fell in love." With both hands, he lifted her face upward. "I can't force you to stay, but I can try to make you fall in love so that your decision to leave will be difficult."

His face lost the nervous expression and changed to one of tenderness. His hands still held her head only now his thumbs brushed lightly against her cheeks. It gave her goosebumps.

"Last night was without doubt the most stimulated I've felt in a long time," he continued. "Yet, in the same breath, I was afraid I might be pushing you into a relationship you didn't want. The disparities between us are wide, Alexandra. You are a gifted surgeon who can do wonderful things for people. I am only a caretaker. My home is here on this mountain while yours can be anywhere in the world." His fingers slipped into her hair. "I want to give you a reason to stay. Would you allow me the chance to make you fall in love?"

She nodded stupidly. She really didn't know what to say.

Charles kissed her tenderly. His mouth suckled and tasted without waiting for her to respond since she couldn't. He walked to the table and grabbed the wine bottle, uncorked it, and poured. His hand shook when he handed her a glass. She took it with one hand while the other touched his to calm it down.

He gave her a weak grin. "I haven't felt so strongly toward a woman for a long time. I'm a nervous wreck. Please bear with me."

"You're doing fine." *Yeah, real words of wisdom.* She said it to soothe his nerves. It did nothing for the grasshoppers in her gut. "You caught me off-guard, Charles."

"Truthfully, you caught me off-guard, too. I thought I steeled myself sufficiently to never fall in love again. Then you come onto the mountain, and I fell faster than a brick."

Alex nearly choked on her wine. She came up gasping, eyes wide. She stared. *"You're in love with me?"*

He returned the stare, his face reflecting the annoyance that surfaced. "Hell, yes! What did you think that speech was all about?"

"You said everyone fell in love with me, not you."

"Well, I'm at the top of the list because no one loves you the way I do. You grabbed my heart the moment you bounced into my back on that very first day. You looked so damn cute."

"You never gave any indication that you were in love with me."

"I couldn't really say it after knowing you for only a few days. You wouldn't believe me. Frankly, I didn't believe it myself, but if you leave tomorrow, you at least know where I stand even at the risk of making a fool out of myself."

"Wow!" She backed away. "I'm stunned. I never saw this coming. What about Sharon?"

A puzzled face stared back. "Sharon?"

"Your girlfriend. The woman who doesn't want me on this mountain."

"We're friends. We grew up together. There is nothing more to it than that. Her family and my family have been on this mountain for eons."

"There's nothing between you two?"

"Other than friendship, no." He refilled her wine glass.

"Maybe you should tell her this piece of news."

He shook his head. "I'm not here to talk about Sharon, or anyone else for that matter. My main focus is you. Just you."

Wow again. She was beyond flattered, beyond stunned. She failed to analyze what rolled around inside her. Fear? Joy? Terror?

"Say something, Alex."

"Are we really going to look at the sky?"

"Of course. What did you think that I was going to

get you drunk and have my way with you?"

"Something like that." Nice thought.

He wagged a finger. "Whatever happens between us, Alexandra Colter, I want you to be a willing participant. Remember what I said today about depth of feeling. There is no better feeling then having sex when love is involved. None of this physical need shit between us. It's cold and mechanical. Understand?"

Alex gasped. "I thought your speech was because you *didn't* love me!"

His eyes turned into slits. "I should have known you would be too damn dense to figure it out. Yes, I'm the one in love; you are not, but that's why I'm here. Now, let me impress you with some stars in the sky."

He talked like a teacher, pointing out bright stars, and patiently showing her constellations. They stood on their feet because they rotated as he talked. To her joy, several meteors shot by. She jumped around like a little kid when she saw them. They drank wine; they munched on cheese and crackers. He played his role as teacher with a great deal of sincerity, making it the most unusual date in her book. Despite her determination not to touch him, he affected her anyway. His voice. His presence. She wanted him, even more than she cared to admit. When she needed to catch her breath and regain some control, she stopped to smell the roses. No man went through so much trouble before. She never noticed if one tried.

She fingered a delicate red rose. "Charles, I don't know what love feels like."

He studied her over his wine glass. "You love Lucy."

"That's different."

"So what you're telling me is you don't know what it feels like to be in love with a man."

She nodded. Over 30 years old and never been in love. Her parents dragged her out of a cave. "I'm scared."

"Of me?"

"Of the unknown."

Charles took both their glasses and placed them on the table. Taking hold of her hand, he sat on the bench and eased her onto his lap. "Let me tell you how I feel. I get breathless every time I look into your eyes. My heart races whenever you stand close. I want to be with you every second of the day and feel absolutely frustrated when I can't. I want to hold and kiss you and call you mine. Most of all, I want to make love to you until the day I die. Should I go on?"

Their eyes locked. Their lips connected simultaneously with such force, she swore he would not allow her to come up for air. His tongue danced with hers while his large hand massaged her ass and pressed her hip against his hard erection. His hand slipped under her jacket and sweater, found her breast, and toyed with the hard nipple. Damn, the man was an absolute turn-on! She wanted to drag him inside the cabin and rip off his clothes.

Unless, of course, he wanted to do it here on the bench.

Fine with her.

His hand slipped between her legs. Even through her blue jeans, his slow massage set her hormones in a rage. She wanted that man's hand against her skin. She reached to undo her zipper when everything stopped. Boom. Done. She looked at him with surprise. He looked back with a very passionate gaze. "I'm not going to rush you. I want you to set the pace. Are you cold?"

"Not now!"

His smile was brief and strained. "I love you very much. I love you so much I'm willing to wait. For now, we'll call it a night. It's late, and the air is noticeably colder. Help me pack up."

Was he kidding? Did he really expect her to turn herself off as easily as he did? What was she, a light bulb?

"Charles, stop. You can't keep doing this to me. You turn me on and then discard me. I can't keep up this emotional roller coaster. Some of us have this physical need shit that you choose to ignore."

He was already on his feet having carefully deposited her on the bench. He turned and watched her steadily. "No, not yet."

Damn him! Those two words again. She laid on the bench and covered her eyes with her forearm. She wanted to shut him out, forget he caused such turmoil. The man liked games, and she was not in the mood. "What do you want from me, Charles?"

"Nothing...and everything."

Great. Riddles, too.

"Are you going to help me?" he asked.

"No." As soon as she said the word, she regretted it. She stood to her feet and grabbed the cheese plate and vase of roses. He gathered what remained including the little red lanterns and placed them in the bed of the truck. The roses and cheese she carried into the cabin. She stood in the kitchen fuming, debating whether to thank him or kick him in the ass. She shook herself instead, counted to twenty, and then scratched her scalp, not giving a fig what it did to her hair. The damn man had her so moist, she wasn't sure if it seeped through her jeans! She stepped out onto the porch to see him standing there with the wine bottle in his hand. He handed it to her. She put it inside before she cracked it over his head. When she returned, he stood by his truck door, hands in his jacket pockets, eyes searching her face. She approached.

"You're leaving me sexually frustrated again." She sighed heavily. "I'll thank you anyway for an interesting evening." No smile. He didn't deserve one. She turned back toward the cabin.

"Do you remember when I stated that the next woman I take to bed will be my wife?"

She turned around. "Changed your mind?"

"No, I said it because I want that woman to love me as much as I love her, and I love you very much."

She jerked. "You want me to be *your wife*? Charles, you can't be serious! We hardly know each other!"

"I know I love you. I will allow you sufficient time to fall in love with me—provided you like me a little."

"A little?" She blinked at him. Actually, she blinked quite a few times. She more than liked him. She didn't want him to leave. She felt the need she had for him, a stirring that was new and foreign and wonderful. She wanted him to hold and kiss her and melt all her bones. She also wanted to feel him inside her. She wanted to feel all he had to give. More than any man before, she wanted him to stay.

My God! The man stirred up feelings of love, a sense of longing, an incredible sense of trust. She *knew* this man would be there no matter what. She *knew* this man would come looking for her if she never showed up. She also knew she would never be alone again because she hadn't felt alone since she arrived. The dismal loneliness that was her constant companion in New York was nowhere to be found on this mountain.

Well, I'll be damned. She stared at him for the longest time. "I love you." She said it so softly, she wasn't sure the words came out of her mouth.

He jerked noticeably but remained where he stood. "How do you figure?"

"I've been in love with you. I never realized it until now." She met his eyes. "You knew, didn't you?"

"Yes."

He moved as if a springboard catapulted him into the air. His arms grabbed her and wrapped tight, pressing her soft breasts to his rock chest with a fierceness that knocked the air out of her lungs. His lips came down with a passion that took only seconds to overwhelm. All his pent-up emotions poured out. She had no experience fighting so powerful a flow. She buckled.

He swept her up into his arms. "I'm not going to let you go," he whispered.

"I don't want you to." She pulled away from his lips and touched his cheek. "Please stay."

He flashed an incredible smile. His whole face lit up from it. "I thought you'd never ask."

"I don't have any condoms."

"I've got eight burning a hole in my pocket. Think that's enough?"

No, but she only kissed him in answer. Still carrying her, he walked over to the bed of the truck.

"Reach in and grab that bag."

She obeyed. She held up the bag and cocked an eyebrow in question.

"Breakfast," he said.

Yeah, breakfast. He thought of everything.

Chapter Sixteen

Charles made up his mind to carry her straight to the bed if she didn't send him away. He prayed she wouldn't. From the moment she arrived on the mountain, he dreamt of this moment, and he could hardly control his greed. He fell in love so quickly. He doubted the feelings she stirred in him, doubted that they were real. The love erupted so fast, and he nearly blew it when he categorized her as another self-centered doctor. She proved to be far different from the others. Every day they were together, he fell deeper in love. Now, his dreams were about to come true.

He undressed her slowly, savoring what he saw. He never had any particular preference for a woman's body parts. Ass, breasts, legs. All very nice. However, Alexandra had one body part that drew him like a magnet: her eyes. Her wide brown eyes melted him. Every time he looked into them, he swam with a dazed wonder. Even now. His bones turned to putty. He told her he wanted her to set the pace, but he retracted that as soon as they hit the bed. If they followed her pace, he would be in her by now, and for him, this was a special moment. He wanted to savor every second, touch every inch of skin, taste every curve. He did. With relish. She accused him of slow torture. He liked the sound of that: slow torture. Her eyes did the same to him.

"Charles, will you get the hell out of your damn

clothes!"

"In a minute." He was too enthralled to undress, but she had a right to see him, too. He stood to his feet and stripped.

Her mouth gaped. "You really are an Adonis!"

The compliment pleased him, and he slipped alongside and captured her mouth. Her neck was next. Then to the hard nipples protruding from her small breasts. His hand separated her legs and massaged gently, increasing the moist heat that told of her readiness.

"Charles—"

Her climax was close. Much too fast. His finger entered the moist canal. It activated a spasm she could no longer control. The contractions squeezed around his finger, and she let out a soft cry until her muscles went limp. Her face flushed with a sated glow.

"I would have preferred to feel you and not your finger," she said.

"Oh, you will. I need to bring you back to a frenzy again." He continued the suckling, the massage, the exploration of her body with his tongue. It didn't take long.

"Damn you," she muttered.

He handed her a condom and rolled onto his back. "Put it on me, doctor."

"Oh, God!"

He watched her rip the packet with fingers that shook ever so slightly. "You can do it," he encouraged.

"I can do it all right. I just don't know if I'll get it on in time."

The touch of her fingers sent him reeling. He wasn't sure she would get it on in time either. But she did. He eased her on top.

Stars outside. Fireworks inside. He rocked her gently until they exploded together, and her softness collapsed against his chest. When she finally lifted her head to look at him, a tear fell out of her eye. He panicked. "Did I hurt you?"

"No, no." She took his face in her hands. "You're amazing."

He rolled her onto her back. "I'm also right, aren't I?"

She nodded. "Sex combined with love is a powerful emotion. I never experienced such a strong outpouring of love from one man."

He kissed her. "I love you very much, Alexandra. I'm giving you a reason to stay. I'm also giving you a chance to never be alone again. Are you thinking about it?"

"I'll give you one guess where my mind is." She kissed him back.

Gad, he loved the taste of her. She was soft, she was sexy, and she was in his arms. "I hope you're ready for me, woman. I'm staying all night."

He never stayed overnight in any of the cabins. Usually, he went to a woman's place if she lived alone. They spent the night, sometimes he returned, sometimes he didn't. He never dated any of the guests even though many tried to get him in bed. They were hardly worth the trouble. Alexandra proved otherwise. She was worth every bit of trouble, and he thought of her constantly. He flooded one cabin because of her. What a mess! He couldn't concentrate on cutting wood let alone plumbing.

She deserved to hear his secrets though. He kept so

much from her, but if he told her now, he would destroy years of personal sacrifice. Even at the risk of losing her, she must not know until the time was right.

"Hey, Mr. Lumberjack! You're far away."

He jerked. "What did you call me?"

She grinned playfully. "That's my nickname for you. It fits, don't you think?"

He roared with laughter. He couldn't help it. For the first time in years, his heart felt full. "You were attracted to me from the beginning. Admit it."

"I admit nothing."

He knew she was. He saw it in those expressive brown eyes when they shared coffee and cookies.

"The lumberjack and the doctor," she said dreamily. "It has a certain ring to it."

"I think of you more like a pipsqueak," he said matter-of-factly.

She didn't like the sound of *that* so she jumped on him. That lead to a bout of laughing and giggling and a wrestling match of which, of course, he let her win. That culminated into another round of lovemaking until they both collapsed with wonderful exhaustion.

She fell asleep in his arms. He watched her sleep. Her warm breath blew against his chest. Her hair tickled his skin. He could hold her like this all night, but neither of them thought to throw a log in the stove. The cabin was noticeably cold. He eased her off his chest and slipped out of bed. After throwing a few logs on a dying fire, he reached to turn off the one lamp they left on by the sofa. He hesitated with his hand under the shade, looked at her, saw her looking at him, and left the light burning. He returned to the bed.

"You can turn out the light," she said sleepily.

He took her in his arms. "I won't be able to see you in the dark." He kissed her forehead. "My little Alexandra. Sleep."

"No." She grabbed another condom and ripped it slowly with her teeth. "On your back, big boy."

He watched her take an inordinate amount of time to slip it on. That alone got him hard as a rod. She hopped on top and eased his shaft into her. She rocked, she rotated until her vaginal contractions tightened around him. She let out a soft cry to intermingle with his own, and he thrust himself deep to increase her pleasure. Sated, she fell asleep in his arms.

They ate breakfast around ten. He cooked, she watched. He wore his dress slacks, but his feet and chest remained bare. She sat at the table in a lightweight robe of blue. She looked gorgeous in it.

"I can't picture you sitting at a desk," she said while pouring coffee. "What was your major at Yale?"

"Finance." The word floored her, and her face showed it. He nearly laughed. He placed the plate of eggs and bacon on the table and sat down. "What else do you picture?"

She sipped her coffee, her eyes scanning him thoughtfully. "As a doctor, I see good muscle tone, excellent skin, and no body fat."

He cocked an eyebrow. "What do you see as a woman?"

Her smile was sly, but he caught it. "We should eat first."

She took her time eating, chewing slowly and deliberately. A torture he knew. Payback. The little devil.

"Finished now?" he asked nonchalantly.

She wiped her mouth. "Time for a shower."

"You read my mind."

Her surgical hands were a gift from God himself. She lathered him to near ecstasy.

"I can't hold off this time, sweetheart."

She was ready for him. She rolled on the condom as easily as a pair of gloves.

"Don't wait," she whispered.

He pressed her against the shower wall and penetrated. He damned near shot her through the ceiling.

By one in the afternoon, they finally dressed. He had his rounds to make, and she expected James. He contemplated whether to ask if he could return tonight when he caught her smiling at him. He smiled back.

"You have a nice smile, Charles. Why don't you use it more often?"

"I need a reason to smile. From now on, I'll be walking around with a silly grin on my face. In the meantime, I hope I can concentrate long enough to get some work done." He picked up his jacket. "By the way, there's a dance at the elementary school tomorrow night. I want you to come." He opened the door and started for the truck.

"A dance?" She followed.

He threw his jacket in the cab. "Every three months, we get together for a dance and social in the gymnasium. All our guests are invited. I know for a fact that a lot of people are anxious to meet you."

"Why, because I'm a doctor?"

"No." He touched under her chin. "Everyone wants to meet the woman I fell in love with."

"Charles—"

"Don't worry. No one will ask you medical questions."

"Charles—"

"It's five dollars at the door. Refreshments are included. Want to come?"

"I can't dance."

That stopped him. "I thought all women danced."

"I never learned. I was always too busy working my way through school. I never had time or money to go to a dance."

"Well, now's your chance. I can teach you."

Her eyebrows shot up with surprise. "You can dance?"

"Henrietta handles the refreshments. She limits her dancing because of a bum knee. You can stay with her when you're not with me."

"What do you mean 'not with you'? Do I have to get in line?"

"You'll see when you get there."

She scuffed at the dirt. "Another guy might ask me to dance."

"Not if he wants to remain on this mountain."

She stared blankly. "What's that mean?"

He took her face in his hands and turned it upward. "You're mine, sweetheart. If the folks on this mountain don't know it by now, they will by the end of the dance." He gave her nose a light kiss. "You'll come?"

"Against my better judgment, yes, I'll come—with one stipulation. I did not agree to marry you yet. I don't want a bold announcement made at the dance. Agreed?"

She was different, no doubt about it. Normally, he gave the orders and expected people to follow them.

For a woman so small, she could be a handful.

"Agreed," he said. "I have to ask you to drive yourself because several of us will be there early to set up. Is that all right?"

"No problem. What time?"

"We start at seven and go on till ten. Dress is casual. Blue jeans are fine."

His hands moved from her face to slip down her back. He pressed her close.

"Charles, about last night—"

He watched and waited, uncertainty creeping into his heart.

"I had a very good time."

"Before or after?"

"All of it," she interjected.

That filled him with a sense of pride. He lifted her so that her legs automatically wrapped around his waist. They were now eye level, and they kissed. When their lips separated, she gave him a dreamy look.

"You make all my bones weak," she said.

"That's why I'm holding you like this." He leaned her against the truck and kissed her again. Reluctantly, he eased her to the ground.

"Will you be back tonight?" she asked.

He studied her. Her eyes were full of doubt. Something troubled her. He wondered what it could be. "Yes, I'll be back tonight. However, I want you to give some serious thought about staying with us on the mountain. I gave you a reason to stay. Whether you choose to accept it, will be your decision." He stepped into the truck. He hesitated before turning the key in the ignition. He looked at her. "I love you, Alexandra. Whatever your decision, I will accept it." His hand reached out the window and gripped her sweatshirt. He pulled her toward the open window for another kiss. Afterwards, he said, "This is one of those times when I wish all the other cabins were unoccupied." His callused finger stroked across her jaw line. "I never had such a fantastic night on this mountain as I had with you, Alex. I want you for a lifetime."

He started down the drive while watching her in the rearview mirror. Alexandra Colter must remain on the mountain. He needed to ensure she didn't follow the same path as his other women.

Chapter Seventeen

James pulled up around three. He came to the door in a freshly starched cop uniform while holding a covered casserole dish.

"It's from Mrs. O'Reilly," he said. "Shepherd's pie. She said to just heat it up."

Homemade food! Her mouth watered when she took a sniff.

"She tells me you can't cook."

Alex groaned. "That tidbit of info must be all over the mountain by now." She put the casserole in the fridge.

"You keep up what you did for Michael's dog, and you'll never have to cook again. I can't cook worth a damn and my fridge is always full." He looked around quickly. "Where do you want me?"

"The table's fine."

"I wanted you to say the bed, but I guess that was wishful thinking."

She smiled. "Sit down, James."

She was unsure how to approach on the subject of Lucy. They were still two strangers, and strangers rarely sat down to have a casual little chitchat over a sensitive subject like paternity. "All right, let me see your arm."

He'd already rolled up his sleeve. She unwrapped the gauze. Careful inspection revealed a clean wound with no seepage and minimal redness. "Are you taking the antibiotics?"

"Yes, Henrietta had them in stock." He studied his arm. "The cut looks good, Doc. I'm glad you were here."

"You were never in any danger. The knife cut through your muscle in one clean slice, missing both arteries in your forearm. I'm more concerned about infection than anything else, but the antibiotics should take care of it." She rewrapped his arm with fresh gauze. Then she played doctor again and felt his forehead. His blue eyes twinkled up at her. "You're flirting with the doctor, Mr. Whatever-the-hell-your-name-is."

"Thomas."

"Right. Mr. Thomas."

"You can't tell me a man hasn't flirted with you before."

"Up until this vacation, I never noticed. I guess I'm improving."

"You're absolutely stunning." He said it with an exaggerated sigh.

She frowned to hide a smile. "Do you have a thermometer?"

"No, why?"

"Would you know how to use it if you got one?"

"I guess Henrietta can show me."

"Then get one. I need to know if you're running a fever."

"Okay." He rolled down his sleeve.

She lifted his chin to see his eyes—even if they twinkled. Yes, they were Lucy's eyes without question. "Did anyone ever tell you that you and Lucy could pass as father and daughter?"

She said it lightly, hoping for some sort of reaction but not the one he gave her. Tears immediately welled up.

"Even a stranger sees it," he said sadly.

"The gold specks are the giveaway, James. I don't need an MD after my name to see the similarity." She sat opposite him at the table.

He sniffed. "Henrietta told me she's talking now."

"Yes, a regular little chatterbox."

"It's your doing. Henrietta swears up and down that you're some kind of miracle worker."

Alex shook her head. "Lucy's voice was always there. She just needed a friend to help break her out of her shell."

"All of us are her friends."

"No, you are adults looking after her. I was there only as a friend." She took one of his hands in both of hers. "She needs you, James."

"Oh, God!" The tears rolled freely down his cheeks. He wiped them away with the back of his hand. "I loved Cindy so much." He sniffed. "Her husband was the scum of the earth, a real bastard in the true sense of the word. I swore I would kill him one day because he constantly beat her. I even took him out in the woods and beat the crap out of him."

"I guess it didn't work."

"No, it only stopped the physical abuse. The mental and emotional abuse continued." Another sniff. "As Lucy got older, it became obvious that she wasn't Tom's daughter, but Cindy made me promise not to interfere. For Lucy's sake. Finally, Cindy had enough and initiated divorce proceedings. I begged her to get a restraining order to keep him away, but of course, she refused. All this was just before the accident. We hadn't a shred of proof that it was anything other than an accident." He said the last statement with a great deal of bitterness.

"You have an eye witness who knows for certain that it was no accident," she told him. "It shocked me to hear such a vivid memory from so young a child."

His blue eyes flashed. "What did she say?"

Alex told him in detail. His jaw tightened, his nostrils flared. She expected flames to burst out of his ears. He shot to his feet nearly toppling the chair. "I should have killed him! All of us on this mountain were convinced that bastard drove the car over the cliff. We couldn't prove it." He paced, furious. "I should have killed him."

"We wouldn't be having his conversation if you did."

That stopped him. "No, I'd be locked up in a state prison."

"And Lucy would still be without a father."

That really calmed him down. He ran a hand through his blond hair, not caring in the least that it stuck out in all directions. "When we found Lucy alive, I was overjoyed. Yet, at the same time, I was sick because the woman I loved was dead." He looked at Alex, his face pleading. "How am I supposed to tell Lucy that I'm her real father after all these years? She'll never believe me."

"She already knows Tom wasn't her father. As she grows older, she'll be curious to find her biological father, and trust me, James, all she has to do is look in the mirror. She's the spitting image of you. Right now, she's too young to see it. So don't you think it would be better to tell her before she resents all the years that passed without you?"

He flopped back onto the chair. "I'm afraid she'll reject me."

"She's five years old, an impressionable little girl. And she already likes you."

His blond brows rose comically. "She does?"

"She told me herself; I'm not making it up." She stood to her feet. "Want a cup of coffee?"

"I'd love one."

"If you're hungry, we can eat the casserole."

"I never refuse good food. That old woman can cook, I'll tell ya."

"See? You're not hard to please. You and Lucy will get along fine. You may need to learn how to cook though." She poured coffee into two cups and handed him one.

"I have no experience being a parent."

"Me neither." She put the casserole in the microwave then took out plates and utensils.

"You're a woman. Somehow, it's natural."

"It's natural because women are gentle. That's all you have to remember with Lucy: be gentle but firm. Love her but give her freedom. Show her discipline but teach her independence."

"You're being philosophical."

"Yes, I know. My display of brains for the day." The casserole was ready. She took it from the microwave and placed it on the table. She handed James a spoon. "Here, fill your own plate."

"I need to blow my nose first."

He did and wiped his eyes. Mr. Gorgeous without a

doubt, even with red swollen eyes.

They ate and talked casually, commenting on the food, the weather, and anything else that came to mind until a silence fell over the table.

She looked up to see him watching her. "Something wrong?"

He toyed with his food. "I want to talk to you about the two bodies we found."

She wondered if he would bring it up. She had a growing curiosity with so many unanswered questions but hesitated to ask. "Charles said he knew them."

"Yes, we knew them. The coroner gave us a confirmed ID when I told him what to look for. You were right about the head wounds being identical. It was the cause of death in both cases." He sipped his coffee. "The wounds were created by a solid object, possibly a baseball bat, delivered by a tall person because of the position of the wound at the top of the head. A lot of strength was involved, too. It was a single blow that killed them."

She shuddered. "Everyone around here seems to be tall, James, except Harry. How do you know the victim wasn't kneeling?"

"No evidence of them being on their knees."

"You said there was a third?"

"We are convinced there is a third, yes. We haven't found any trace of her yet."

"And you're telling me this because?"

He watched her steadily, his face serious, his eyes cautious. Finally, he said, "All three women dated Charles."

He could have stabbed her with his fork. She sat back, stunned. "What are you telling me, that you suspect Charles?"

"I have no evidence to point at one particular person. The evidence is circumstantial to say the least."

Alex's mind raced. She just spent an unforgettable night with an amazing man only to discover he might be a cold-blooded killer? No, it wasn't possible. "What's your gut feeling, James?"

He pushed his plate aside. "I have my suspicions, but no proof. Is Charles innocent in all this? I don't know. A very powerful blow killed each of those two women. One hit. Instantaneous death. I'm telling you this for your own safety. You could be the next victim."

"*Me*! Why—because of Charles?"

"Yes, because of Charles. I need you to keep your ears and eyes open. Don't hesitate to call me for any reason."

"Maybe I should just go back to New York."

He grabbed her forearm. "That's exactly what I don't want you to do. I have to catch this killer. The future of our mountain depends on it."

She groaned and retracted her arm. "You're using me as bait, James. I could wind up dead."

"I'm going to do everything in my power to prevent that. In the meantime, I don't want you to talk about this to anyone, not even Charles. Is that clear?"

"How do I know you're innocent? You're tall and could easily have struck those women."

"True. I have only my word to give you."

She shook her head. "I should just leave."

"No, you're not leaving until you help me with Lucy."

She looked at him suspiciously. "You're asking a bit much of me, Officer Thomas. What am I supposed

169

to do with Lucy?"

"I can't simply walk up to her and say, 'Hey, kid, I'm your dad!' You have a way with people, Alex, especially Lucy. Have a confab with her. See how receptive she is. Please."

Oh, damn! She'd stuck her foot in quicksand this time. "All right, all right, I'll give it a try. When?"

"How about now?"

He would say that. She rose to put their plates in the sink. "I'll have to find her first." Too much information too fast. She couldn't take her mind off the news about Charles let alone try to concentrate on Lucy. She ran her fingers through her hair. She glanced over at James to find his gaze pleading. Like she had all the answers. "I really don't know what to say, James."

"You'll find the words. What time should we meet?"

Alex studied the kitchen clock. "Arrange to be at the general store by five. This will give me enough time to find her and talk. We'll wing it from there."

"She might not want to meet me."

"It's possible. She might not be ready. In either case, you should be at your charming best. If we're not there, that means she isn't ready."

James shot to his feet, this time from nervous energy. He wrung his hands. "I've waited for this day, waited a long time, wondering, hoping she would accept me. Look!" He shoved his hands close to her face. "My palms are sweating!"

"That's from your coffee cup."

"No, it isn't. I'm scared to death!"

The man took two decomposed bodies off the mountain, and beat a criminal to a pulp with one hand, yet he was afraid of a little girl? Alex smiled at him. "We'll give it a try and see what happens."

They headed to the door. Fellow conspirators.

"Make sure to watch your back, Alex. And remember, not a word about our conversation."

"Just one question. Was Charles in love with any of the victims?"

He rubbed the back of his neck while a frown scrunched up his face. "I can't answer that for sure. They weren't serious relationships, just women he met in the valley." He dropped his hand. "Why?"

"Why were the women killed here on Billings Mountain where they would eventually be found? Why not kill them in the valley? Charles loves this mountain. I doubt he would do anything to draw negative attention to it."

He studied her. "You believe he's innocent?"

"Of course I do. Don't you?"

"I'm praying he has nothing to do with this."

"And again, James, why here? Why Billings Mountain?"

He frowned as he watched her. "Opportunity," he said simply. "They were here with Charles. That does not exclude him, Alex. It substantiates suspicion."

Concern spread across his face. He wasn't at all sure of Charles' innocence.

Neither was she when she thought about it. "If I wind up dead, I'm coming back to haunt you."

He leaned over for a kiss, a tender kiss on the lips. "You're brave, and you're smart, Dr. Colter. You're going to help me catch this killer, or we both die in the process."

"That's encouraging." She opened the door. "Go

on, get out so I can find Lucy."

There must be something special about these men on Billings Mountain. James was a pretty good kisser, too.

Chapter Eighteen

Alexandra's interpretation of a vacation involved fun activities. Hiking, exploring and visiting new places, museums. All fun activities. Uniting a father and daughter? Not on the fun list. Examining dead bodies? Not on the fun list either. Two dead women, a third yet to be found. All dated Charles. She wanted to say "a coincidence", but she couldn't quite mouth the words. Something was terribly wrong on this mountain, and two dead women were proof.

She should just pack up and leave, get the hell off the mountain, get back to New York and forget she fell in love, forget the people, forget everything that happened.

Yeah, right. She could never forget her week here, nor the man who changed her whole life. He offered companionship, security, a chance to belong. No one ever affected her so quickly, so strongly. He wanted marriage of all things. That one word alone kept her brain absolutely numb. She had trouble tying her boots laces because of him. She zipped up her jacket and started down the path to the general store.

She kept her mind blank as she walked. Talking to a five year old necessitated an entirely different strategy then talking to an adult. A child's brain worked on simple terms. One word to an adult would have a different meaning to a child. She made that startling

173

revelation on her rotation in pediatrics when she was a resident. Therefore, she enjoyed the walk and the crisp mountain air, sucking in fragrances she would never smell once she returned to New York.

It dawned on her—a little late—how Henrietta would feel about all this. Would she be angry? Overjoyed? Or just plain relieved? A woman in her late sixties taking care of an energetic five year old had to be tiring. Couple that with the responsibility of a general store, a post office, a pharmacy, hell, yeah, mind-boggling exhausting.

A remarkable woman this Henrietta Carlson.

Alex paused on the bridge. The stream flowed lazily along in no hurry to get anywhere. Like her. Putting off the inevitable. She leaned over the rail to stare absently down at the water.

She'd seen the bear cubs with the head and alerted Charles. That led them to the first body. She uncovered the scarf by the waterfall, and they found the second body. Would she discover the whereabouts of the third?

"God, I hope not," she said.

A chilly breeze followed the stream and stirred her hair. It brought visions of snow and ice and plows running up and down the mountain road. Even during her short visit, each night brought a noticeable difference in the air. Before long, her jacket won't be warm enough.

"Hi, Alex!" Lucy ran onto the bridge, her Elmo doll in tow. Alex meant what she said to Charles. She would love to take this little girl home with her. "Do you get a lot of snow up here, Lucy?"

"Lots and lots."

She took that with a grain of salt. Two inches

would be lots and lots to a child. "How about snow plows?"

"That's Harry's job. He does our driveway and parking lot."

"Does Mr. Billings pay for it?"

"I don't know."

He probably paid. Technically, the asphalt road was his driveway. "What can you tell me about Mr. Billings?"

"I'm not allowed to talk about him."

That surprised her. "Why?"

Lucy picked up a small twig and tossed it into the stream. "Because."

"That's not a reason. Does he talk to you?"

"Oh, yes."

Alex searched for a bird that squawked up in the trees. It sounded big whatever it was. "Does he go out much?"

"Everyday."

That, too, surprised her. "Where does he go?"

"Anywhere he wants. This is his mountain."

Fair enough. A whole mountain as a realm. He could do hopscotch on the roadway if he wanted. "Is he a nice man?"

"I like him."

"Then that's all that matters." Alex sat on the wooden deck and leaned back against the rails. Lucy copied her, right down to stretching out her legs and wiggling her boots. "Do you remember what you told me yesterday about your dad?"

"Yes."

"And how you found out you weren't his daughter?"

175

"Yes."

"It's true, Lucy. Your mother fell in love with another man, and you were created by that love."

Her blue eyes grew cautious. "How do you know?"

"Your real father told me today how much he loved your mother."

Her mouth fell open. "He's here?"

"Yes, he's here. He's always been here on this mountain."

She frowned, her face thoughtful. "It was wrong, wasn't it, what he and mommy did?"

"Yes, it was wrong."

"Daddy beat her because of me."

"Your father beat your mother long before you came along. So, it wasn't your fault that he hurt her. The man who helped create you told me all about it. He wanted to take you and your mother away."

Lucy looked up. "Why didn't he?"

"Because your mom wouldn't let him. He was very disappointed."

She fell silent. She adjusted Elmo on her lap and wrapped her little arms tight around him. The poor doll's eyes nearly popped out. "Why don't I know who he is?" she asked finally.

"He's afraid you won't like him. He already loves you very much. He has been part of your life since the day you were born."

Her pretty face scrunched together in a pout. "He never said anything."

"No, but now he wants to be your father—if you'll let him."

"I like Henrietta."

"Henrietta will always be there."

Her face brightened. "Maybe she can marry him, and we can all live together."

Alex nearly laughed. "She's a little old for him, Lucy, but you can think of her as a grandmother."

"What about you then?"

Alex brushed a spider off her pant leg. "What?"

"Marry him. Then the three of us can live together. Nobody wants you to leave, Alex. I hear them talking about it all the time."

"Who?"

"Henrietta and Charles and James. We like you and want you to stay."

"I live in a different world, Lucy. I'm not sure I can afford to stay. But your happiness is what I want to concentrate on right now. Do you want to meet your father?"

"Yes." She stood to her feet. "I will meet him. Will you be there?"

"Every step of the way." Alex stood also. "I will introduce you."

"I don't need to be in-tro-duced. He knows me already."

"But you don't know who *he* is."

"Oh. Yeah." She slipped her little hand in Alex's and looked up. "Where we going?"

"To the general store. I asked him to meet us there."

They walked hand-in-hand down the path, neither one of them hurrying. Alex kicked a pile of leaves; Lucy kicked a pile of leaves. Alex picked up a stick and threw it; Lucy picked up a stick and threw it. Her copycat. She loved it.

When they reached the general store, the patrol car

was not there. A black Camaro sat in a slot instead. *Oh, joy.* The last person she wanted to see. Unfortunately, they collided the second she rounded the corner. Alex waited for the inevitable explosion.

"Well, well, Dr. Colter. How nice to see you again."

No explosion but a chilling slice of ice. "Hello, Miss Warner."

By daylight, Sharon Warner was breathtaking. Her fiery red hair hung loosely while sharp emerald eyes glistened with a controlled rage. She had full lips lightly glossed, which even now curled into a sneer.

Controlled rage indeed.

"I'm glad we ran into each other," she said coldly. "I'd like to know if you're staying."

"Staying?"

"You know, on the mountain, setting up a practice."

"It's not on my agenda."

"That's good to hear. Make sure you keep it off your agenda. As for the rest of your list, I suggest you forget it and get your little ass back to New York where you belong." The emeralds turned into cold ice. "I suggest you do it quickly. Charles is not what he appears."

That caught her attention. She eyed her sharply. "What do you mean?"

"He's keeping secrets from you, doctor—secrets he should never keep from a woman. The longer you stay, the more you put your life in danger since his girlfriends have a tendency to disappear. Consider my warning a fair one and get the hell off this mountain." She got in her car and sped off, leaving Alex and Lucy in a cloud of dust.

Lucy tugged on her hand. "She's not very nice."

"Hate to agree with you, but you're right. She is not very nice, especially to me."

"How come?"

Alex shrugged in answer. She wasn't sure she understood it herself. Charles could be burning the candle at both ends, playing one woman against the other. Not a wise move. Sharon was clearly jealous. What were the secrets he kept? Did it have to do with the two dead women? More importantly, how would Sharon know unless they were in it together? She shuddered at the thought.

"What's an a-gen-da?" Lucy asked.

"Something that you plan to do, like you meeting your father." She squatted down to look into her eyes. "We'll go into the store. When he arrives, I'll give you a signal. How's that sound?"

"Okay." Her young face grew thoughtful. "What if I don't like him?"

"Nobody is rushing you into anything, Lucy."

"I'm scared."

"Then remember, he loves you very much, and right now, he's as scared as you."

They walked into the store.

Henrietta stood behind the counter stocking cigarettes. She glanced over her shoulder as they entered. "Well, hi, you two. Been out for a walk?"

"I'm going to meet my father," Lucy stated.

The cigarettes flew. Henrietta's flaring arms struggled to catch them. She gave up and whirled. "Is this true?" she asked.

Oh, dear, please don't get upset. Alex nodded.

Tears welled up in the older woman's eyes. She picked up what she dropped and continued with the stocking. Alex went behind the counter to stop her. "You'll never be able to find anything later," she said gently. She took the cigarettes from her hand and placed them on the counter.

Henrietta grabbed a tissue to dab her eyes. "I wondered how long it would take him to get around to it."

"I hope you don't mind."

"Honey, I've been trying since the accident to get him to step forward. You truly have a magic touch. I'm sorry you weren't here a few minutes ago. Sharon needed some of your calming effect."

"I have no magic touch when it comes to Sharon. The woman hates my guts." She jerked. Did Sharon hate Charles' other girlfriends as well? Was she solely responsible for the murders? It made better sense than the two of them being in cahoots. It's what Alex wanted to believe anyway. "What was she angry about?"

"I've no idea. She and Charles had one of their heated discussions out in the parking lot, but that's normal for them. She came in fuming; she left fuming. I'm surprised she didn't bite my head off."

Two people walked into the store. Alex met them the other night at the star party. They exchanged pleasantries, but her focus was on Lucy. The little girl looked up. Alex shook her head. While Henrietta waited on the couple, Alex poured a cup of coffee. If she had half a brain in her head, she should pour a cup of decaf, but no, she went straight for high test. She already shook from nervousness. Another shot of caffeine should send her right up a pole.

She drank it anyway.

A man walked in. Lucy looked aghast and quickly stared up at Alex. Relief flooded the little girl's face when Alex shook her head.

A glance at the clock showed the time at five ten. The store closed at five thirty. Even Henrietta's face reflected worry. Where the hell was he? If that man chickened out, Alex swore she would kick his ass up and down that long mountain road. Luckily, Lucy amused herself by straightening up the magazine rack. Elmo sat perched on the counter, looking nonchalant. Alex poured a second cup of high test.

Finally, the door opened, and James walked in. He'd changed out of his cop uniform into a pale blue shirt and blue jeans. He looked nervous. His eyes darted around the store, looked at Alex, then Henrietta until locking onto Lucy. Lucy glanced up at him but never looked at Alex so used to him coming into the store. She frowned a little. "I wish it were James."

Alex squatted to her eye level. "Lucy, it *is* James."

The little girl's eyes went wide. Then she stared at James. He stood there watching her, looking every bit the nervous expectant father. Like a bolt of lightning, Lucy ran to him. He swept her up in one quick sweep. Two blonde heads came together and stayed that way.

Henrietta stood behind the counter bawling her eyes out. "You are an angel sent from heaven," she said through her tears. "I don't ever want you to leave this mountain."

Henrietta asked the impossible. Even an angel had wings and took flight. Alex kissed her lightly on her wet cheek and quietly left the store.

Chapter Nineteen

Charles returned after she fell asleep. He slipped into bed smelling of pine and freshly cut wood. Alex expected him to initiate lovemaking, but he merely cuddled her close to his chest. By morning, his large hand cupped her femininity and massaged in a way only a man could do, slow with just the right touch of pressure. She reached over to give him equal pleasure only to discover his shaft up and ready. He entered her, on top this time, his movements deep and rhythmic. She gave herself to him completely until his thrust popped her eyes open with a gasp. They climaxed together, but he wasn't finished. He suckled her breasts while his hand continued its magical skill. Arousal returned. His penetration followed, thrusting deep within her. She cried out in sheer pleasure. No man had ever taken such time with her, and she knew without doubt that she loved this man very much. He kissed her back to sleep. She woke a few hours later, alone, with the smell of coffee.

Before she got her boots on for one last hike up the mountain, Lucy came to the door. In her arms, she carried a new coffee maker still in its box. She carried it with care, her little arms struggling to keep the box close to her chest. She handed it over with pride.

"What's this?" Alex asked.

"Charles said you needed a new one."

"Why? There's nothing wrong with the one I have."

"He told me to tell you not to yell at the messenger."

Alex laughed. "All right, thank you, Miss Lucy. Where's Elmo?"

"I couldn't carry him, too. I promised Henrietta I wouldn't drop the box."

"Well, come in, Miss—what is your last name anyway?"

"It's going to be Thomas. James said I should start calling myself that because he's gonna talk to lawyers about changing my name." She thought a moment. "I guess I should start calling him Daddy."

"I'm sure he will love it. If he doesn't, he will have to answer to me."

She giggled with that and climbed onto a kitchen chair while Alex unpacked the coffee maker. Charles said she needed a new one? She looked at the one on the counter. Aside from heavy use, it looked okay unless he saw the tiny knick on the glass rim, and the plastic lid had a small crack, and the burner and outer casing was stained...well, maybe it was time for a new one.

"Henrietta won't let me drink coffee," Lucy said.

"Very wise of her."

"She lets me drink tea though."

"Then would you like a cup of tea with me?"

"I'd love it, Doc-torr Col-torr."

Alex smiled at the way she pronounced her name. "I have some cookies so we will have a few with our tea. You can tell Henrietta that you had a morning tea with me."

"Like the British?"

"Like the British." She already had water boiling since she wanted to take tea in the thermos. She made two cups and handed one to Lucy. "Here's your tea, Miss Thomas. Let it cool a bit before you drink it. And don't eat too many cookies. I don't want Henrietta yelling at me for spoiling your lunch."

Alexandra joined Lucy at the table with her own cup of tea. Lucy acted very ladylike. She put in a little sugar then a little cream, stirring ever so slowly. She blew on a spoonful for two minutes then took a sip. When Alex dunked her cookie, she followed suit but left it in the hot fluid too long. The cookie broke and fell in.

"Oh, drat!"

"I'll bet it tastes much better now that it's fully soaked," Alex said. "Spoon it out and see."

Lucy looked at her suspiciously.

"Would I lie to you?"

"No." She spooned out her soggy cookie and blew on it.

Finally, the moment of truth. She ate it. "Yes, it tastes much better."

"See. Told you so. Now, tell me what arrangements James made for you."

"He says he needs to clean out his bach-o-lor pad first. Then he's giving me my own room. I asked him to make a room for you, but he said you were already spoken for."

"That isn't definite yet. Tell him not to jump to conclusions."

"Are you coming to the dance tonight?" she asked.

"Yes, I'll be there. I can't dance though."

"Me neither, but James—I mean Daddy—said he would teach me. Maybe he can teach you, too."

"I need all the help I can get." *And then some*. She also might need a sedative.

"This is my very first dance," Lucy said proudly.

"Believe it or not, it will be my first one, too."

Lucy peered with suspicious eyes. "That doesn't sound right. You're old."

"I'm thirty-one! That's not old!"

Lucy giggled and daintily sipped her tea.

A short time later, Alex raced Lucy home. Because she felt like it, she ran all the way back.

Old indeed.

****

Alex set off up the mountain with one purpose in mind: to see the Billings Mansion again. For possibly the last time. If the outcome tonight went as expected, she would never be able to return.

She made a decision to leave. Just before she went to bed last night, she wrote out a list of pros and cons whether she should stay, whether to go. Ultimately, as expected, the list lacked one very important detail: money. Charles offered, but she had no desire to deplete his bank account because of career responsibilities. Therefore, her best option was to return to New York to accumulate cash, pay down debt, and save enough to set up a practice on the mountain. Her biggest obstacle was Charles. He already stated that he wouldn't wait. If he stubbornly refused to change his mind, she would remain in New York and forget about this extraordinary man who entered her life and altered it forever. She should tell him tonight after the dance. The man needed a quick education about the business of being a doctor.

Gad, it would hurt like hell. For her. For him. She wanted so much to stay, but how could she possibly pay her bills? She struggled all her life. She may struggle all the way till death. Life would have been a lot simpler if she just flipped burgers for a living.

She nearly wrote out another list while she was at it. A list of secrets. Everyone on this damn mountain harbored a secret: Lucy, James, Sharon, and now, Charles. Who was next, Henrietta? Or how about Harry? And who the hell was Billings? If he went out every day, why haven't they met and why was he so friggin' secretive?

Alex followed the asphalt road uphill until it ended at the Billings house. The grounds were deserted. No gardener. No one on the porch. No cars in the drive. Absolutely no one about. She boldly took a few steps into the circular drive to get a better view of the house.

The mansion stood white and glorious under a bright autumn sun. It had to be visible for miles down in the valley. White among the green, unobstructed in all directions. Toward the north side of the porch in the back corner, a round dome popped up looking totally out of place. An observatory without question. At the top of the house, dead center, was a rectangular deck surrounded by ornate gingerbread railings. She wouldn't hesitate for a second to sit up there on a lounge chair. A seat at the top of the world—literally. Fantastic, unobstructed views in all directions.

As she stood there gawking, a woman walked out the front door carrying a broom. She immediately set to work, sweeping briskly across the porch. At this distance, Alex couldn't see her face, but her first impression was a woman in her early seventies. Possibly the housekeeper. Or maybe Billings' wife. She matched the age of the man she saw on her last visit. The woman used the broom with skill while working her way toward the wide staircase. She suddenly caught sight of Alexandra and stopped. Alex gave a shy little wave and turned to leave only to see Harry standing behind her.

"Fancy meeting you here," he said cheerfully.

"You said that the last time we met." She looked down the road. "Where's your truck?"

"I'm out for a walk today. Admiring the house?"

She turned toward it. "I've never seen anything quite so fascinating."

"Too big and old for me, not like my garage is a palace. That's the Billings house."

"So I've been told. I hope I didn't set off any alarms."

"Nay. Lots of guests gawk at the place. Some people are brazen enough to go up to the front door and knock. That's Greta Tillerman on the porch." He waved. "She's the housekeeper. Been there for ages."

The woman leaned on the broom and stared. "She looks the type who can handle anyone coming to the door," Alex said. "How many people live here?"

"Only four. A niece and nephew come to stay with Greta every now and then. Billings himself has no family. If he doesn't correct that problem, it will be the end of us."

She looked at him, puzzled. "Why?"

"No heirs. If he doesn't marry and have a bunch of kids, this place will turn into a hotel, and all our lives will change."

"Too bad," she said seriously. It pained her to think of the manor house as a hotel. Then again, if it was a hotel, she could book a room. "What's the guy like?"

"Besides being filthy rich?" He chuckled softly. "He's a cantankerous old buzzard. Too set in his ways for my liking. He'd probably give you a tour if you asked."

"I'd love to see the inside."

His hazel eyes got very bright behind the wire-rimmed glasses. "Seems to me you're already in love with the place."

"I am, but I won't impose. I can hardly expect Billings to give me a tour when I've never met the guy."

Harry ran a hand through his spiked hair. It stayed spiked. "It's rare if he introduces himself to one of our guests. He likes the anonymity of wandering around without anyone knowing whether he lives on the mountain or is a guest." He nodded toward the house. "He might make an exception for you especially if he hears you fell in love with this monstrosity."

"Don't call it that. It's an old manor house—I think."

"Yes, it is. Most is original except for part of the back. There was a fire in the early 1900's that destroyed the north section. The front is still original. Billings is very proud of the place. Anyone who has lived on this mountain for any length of time has seen the inside. It's nice, more modern than the outside. At least you don't feel like you walked into a museum."

She wouldn't care. Even a museum was better than her shit-hole of an apartment in New York. She cut corners a little too much with that place. "Lucy told me

Billings goes out every day."

"Yep, he's out rain or shine always checking his mountain."

"He has James for that."

"Yeah—well, he must think James has a million things to do. A domestic one day. A fist fight another. The guy who knifed him was an exception as far as excitement is concerned. When the tourists flock here in the spring, we get busier and most of that is car trouble. Shall we walk back together?"

She welcomed the suggestion. All the way up, she kept looking over her shoulder for the black Camaro. "Sharon told James she lost control around the curve." She glanced at him. "Do you believe that?"

He looked at her thoughtfully. "Do you?"

"Not by a long shot, but James is right. It's her word against mine."

They started down the asphalt road. Harry gave a history of every house they passed: who built it, who owned it, the renovations made. He talked of plant life and animal life with a proud hint in his voice. She wondered if he was the elusive H.C. Billings. Why else would he be on foot just out for a walk when he had a garage to tend to? Then again, why would he get his nails all greasy working in a garage if he was filthy rich?

Logic won. The man couldn't possibly be H.C. Billings.

When they reached the overlook, she stopped and stared at the view with a sigh. "I do love it here. I never realized how much until now."

Harry leaned up against the stone wall to face her. "Then stay."

"I can't."

"I thought you and Charles were hitting it off. You do love the big lug, don't you?"

"Yes, very much, but that's not the problem. I have a huge loan to pay off. I can't make any money here." She leaned against the parapet. "I thought long and hard about this, Harry. I have to sacrifice the love I feel here to do what's right. I'll leave tomorrow."

He jerked. "Dear Lord, you'll break his heart!"

She faced him. "I don't want it to be permanent, but I know he won't wait." She paused, deep in thought. She already knew the answer to her next question, but she asked anyway. "Do you think Charles will leave the mountain?"

"Hell, no, not even in a coffin. He wants his ashes scattered over the shrubs to help fertilize them. He won't want you to leave either."

"I've no choice. The big bucks are in New York. I'll talk to him after the dance."

Harry's face reflected his concern. "None of us want you to leave, Alex. For some strange reason, we believe you belong here."

"And the mountain will finally have a doctor."

"No. As much as we need a doctor, that isn't the reason we want you to stay. You captivated Charles. It's been a long time since he fell in love. We're happy because you're the one he fell in love with. He might make an offer if it's cash you need."

"It is cash, and he already made an offer. I won't take it because I know it won't be enough. My only other option is to work as a staff surgeon in a hospital down in the valley."

"He won't like that idea. It's too far."

"Well, I won't take his money. In the meantime, I have a guaranteed job in New York. I'll talk to him tonight." She touched his arm. "Don't tell anyone of my decision to leave—please."

"I won't. I'm hoping the dance changes your mind. Charles is a very good dancer."

Alex groaned.

"What's the matter?"

"I can't dance."

He laughed. "So much for Fred Astaire romancing Ginger Rogers."

Chapter Twenty

Alexandra sat in the school parking lot unwilling to step out of the car. She counted the people going in, saw that no one came out, yet she sat, too terrified to move. This was the dance, her moment of truth. She didn't want to be here, didn't want to come, would rather break a leg and use it as an excuse.

Oh, how bad could it be? Pretty bad when she thought about it. She forced her ass out of the car.

A crowd hung around the double doors to the school entrance, mostly smokers looking like a cluster of chimneys. They were boisterous, all talking at once, some laughing. They got noticeably quiet as she approached. Every face turned. Smiles spread easily, their greetings polite and friendly. The stranger among them.

"The doctor is here!" someone proclaimed. "Hide the cigarettes!"

Like little kids, they whipped their cigarettes behind their backs and grinned. She laughed and walked through the double doors.

Inside the entrance hall, an elderly man sat at a table with a cash box in front of him. Another man, Harry, obviously just arrived. He removed a lightweight jacket and sat down. Both looked up as she approached. "You must be Dr. Colter," The man stood. "I'm Sam Gibson. I run the small engine repair shop on the mountain. Everyone is pleased as punch that you agreed to attend our dance." He extended his hand. "This here is—"

"She knows me," Harry said with a smile.

"Yes, hi, Harry." She shook both their hands.

Harry was slightly out of breath. He was also flushed. He had the look of a man who just ran a mile. The gas station was no more than 200 yards down the road.

Maybe he needed a cardiac workup.

"Charles took care of you, Doc. You don't owe us a dime."

Good. He should pay. He invited her to this damn dance. She put her money back in her jeans pocket.

Not everyone would be pleased as punch to see her. One woman in particular should boil with rage. If Charles was here, then Sharon was here. *Gee whiz, can't wait. What words of wisdom will the woman pass on tonight?* Alex entered the gymnasium.

The place vibrated with noise, movement, and music. The same hyperactive kids from the star party ran around the gym like a train off its tracks, colliding into older residents who looked ready to strangle them. People of all ages danced. Those standing around saw her enter and stared. Several women walked over to introduce themselves and shake her hand. She didn't catch any of their names. She did catch the array of gasps and comments.

Embarrassing as hell. They acted as if a celebrity had the graciousness to stop by to say hello. She returned their smiles and shook many hands all the while trying to break through a crowd that got thicker. An older woman rushed over and plowed her way through. Alex recognized her from this morning.

"I'm Greta Tillerman." She eagerly pumped Alex's hand. "I'm Mr. Billings' housekeeper. Do you like the house?"

"I think it's fascinating."

"I'm sure Mr. Billings wouldn't mind if I gave you a tour. He's so proud of the place. In fact, he's proud of the whole mountain."

"He should be. It's very nice up here." Whoever the hell he was.

"Then stop by tomorrow. I'll show you around."

Several more people came over to pump her hand. Out of the corner of her eye, she saw Henrietta standing behind a long wooden table loaded with food and beverages. She waved her over. Alex didn't hesitate a second.

"You're late," she yelled over the music.

"It's only eight."

"Charles has been looking for you for the past hour."

"He doesn't even know I'm here."

"Don't kid yourself, honey. He saw you the second you walked through the door."

Alex scanned the couples on the dance floor. James and Lucy danced together. Lucy stood on his shoes as he moved with the music. They both gave her a wave. Charles was dancing with Marge. He flashed Alex a smile and a wink but politely kept his attention on Marge.

Eyes still followed her. Even from the dance floor, people stared, some with smiles, others with faces full of curiosity.

"You may as well be on center stage," Henrietta

said. "Everyone wants to see the woman Charles fell in love with."

"I don't understand what the big deal is."

"We're family, Alexandra. All these people will be at your wedding."

Four people walked over, introduced themselves, and shook her hand. One woman had tears in her eyes. When they left, Alex turned back to Henrietta. "These people are acting like I accepted."

"It's a given, dear, and everyone knows it. Charles hasn't been the same since you drove onto the mountain."

Alex looked at all the happy faces smiling at her from the dance floor. Their attention was getting a trifle uncomfortable. "I don't know why I'm here," she groaned. "I can't dance."

"You're here because Charles invited you. There is no better reason than that." She smiled kindly. "Relax, Alexandra. As soon as the song is over, Charles will make a beeline toward you."

The music stopped. Everyone clapped. Alex waited for the beeline.

"Wow! I'm going deaf!" Henrietta said with an exaggerated shake of her head. "Want something to eat?"

"Not yet." She still waited for that beeline.

Another song started with some fanfare. People applauded and whistled while forming a wide circle around a couple in the middle of the dance floor.

Charles and Sharon.

Oh, joy.

"Watch this," Henrietta said with a face full of anticipation. "These two dance so well together,

195

everyone stops to watch."

She wasn't kidding. The entire gymnasium stood motionless while all eyes remained glued to the lone couple on the dance floor. They were good. Charles and Sharon moved like a professional dance team who spent hours perfecting a flawless routine. They glided across the floor, their steps precise, two people moving as one. The lumberjack was surprisingly light on his feet.

"Sharon looks exceptionally stunning tonight," Henrietta said with a sigh.

Yeah, no shit. While the entire crowd wore casual clothes, Sharon stood out in a flowing green dress that moved with the slightest breeze. It emphasized her sensual moves, time and again showing the green spandex panties underneath. Her legs, long and slender, tapered down to a pair of spiked heels with possibly the pointiest toes on the market. She was clearly overdressed for the crowd. Alex felt sick as she watched them.

"You can learn," Henrietta said.

Alexandra could not respond. She was absolutely, positively out of her league here. Sharon's moves were downright sexy. Instincts told her to bolt straight for the door.

The song ended. The crowd applauded and cheered as the two dancers took a bow. The music started again, and the circle filled with dancers. Charles and Sharon came to the refreshment table, both flushed and happy, hands clasped, still moving as one. Sharon glared at Alex with a look of triumph in her green eyes.

People of all ages approached to congratulate them on a flawless routine. Quite a few turned to Alex to pump her hand as if she were the choreographer.

Sharon seethed after that. Each time Charles stepped toward Alex, Sharon moved with him always keeping herself firmly planted between them. This blatant maneuver aggravated the badger in Alex. She didn't like the tactic one damn bit. She wanted to rip those emerald eyes right out of her head.

After one last try, Charles finally grabbed Sharon by the shoulders and growled something to her face. Her red eyebrows rose halfway up her forehead, and she stepped aside.

A slow song started. Charles took hold of Alex's hand and guided her onto the dance floor. Thankfully, the crowd didn't form a circle to watch.

Eyes followed them anyway.

"My chance to hold you close," he said with a heavy sigh. He was forcing himself to relax, she knew. Sharon did her best to aggravate the both of them. The woman was possessive, no doubt about it.

Charles took her in his arms and pressed her to his chest. "Just flow with me, Alex. We won't do anything fancy."

"Good because I can't compete with Sharon."

"I don't expect you to. Sharon and I grew up together. We had plenty of practice. Look at me."

She looked up.

"You're scared to death!"

"I'm uncomfortable in the limelight doing an activity I've never done. Put a scalpel in my hand and give me a crowd three times this size, and I'll feel right at home. After the way you danced with Sharon, people will look at me and laugh. You're a fabulous dancer by the way."

"Thank you. Sharon and I always put on a show at

these functions. People enjoy it."

"I'm sure they do." He failed to catch the hint of sarcasm in her voice. Just as he failed to notice Sharon boiling by the refreshment table. Sharon wanted Charles. Any woman with cataracts in both eyes and half a brain in her skull could easily see it. Hell, she was like a flashing neon sign!

"What are you thinking?" he asked.

"That I shouldn't be here."

"Nonsense. I love holding you like this. If the music stopped, I wouldn't care. I will still hold you. If you're worried about people commenting on your dancing, then I'll give them something to talk about because I absolutely cannot hold off any longer."

He kissed her, a long, tender, moist kiss full of feeling. He lifted her off her feet in the process, giving the sensation of floating on air. Afterwards, they stood staring into each others eyes neither one caring who was around or whether they watched or not. At this particular moment in time, they were the only two people in the gymnasium.

"I've missed you terribly," he whispered. He kissed her nose. "I'm glad you came."

"Trust me, I debated it, but you just changed my mind." She put her head on his chest. He wore cologne. It seeped through his white shirt and into her nose. Very nice.

"Harry tells me you were up at the Billings house. Do you like that monstrosity?"

"It has a certain charm."

"That's not what you told him."

She looked up. "All right, I love the place. It's unique, it's big, has loads of character. My apartment would fit into that south porch with room to spare. I can't imagine living in such a palace."

He made a face. "I wouldn't call it a palace. The inside is big but ordinary."

"To me, it's a palace. Mrs. Tillerman offered to give me a tour."

"I've a feeling Billings would prefer to give the tour himself. Ancestor home, that sort of thing." He dipped her and smiled at the inevitable shriek.

"I thought you said nothing fancy," she complained.

"I lied." He dipped her again just to show who was in control. "Harry also tells me you're worried about money," he continued. "I don't want you to fret over money, Alex. We should be able to work something out. Maybe consolidate and refinance."

"That's too much of a burden, Charles. I have an expensive profession. I wished they had taught us that before we started med school." She again put her head on his chest. The security of his arms relaxed her. She moved with his gentle rhythm while listening to the heart beating in his chest. That heart belonged to her. She knew it; she felt it. She would not have said this earlier, but right now, she wanted the song to last forever.

"Should I come to the cabin tonight?" he asked. "We can discuss your money problems. I might have a solution."

She needed a miracle, not a solution. She smiled. "Yes, come after the dance."

The music stopped and without skipping a beat, another song started with fanfare. A rough tap on her shoulder forced her to turn. Sharon. Glaring emeralds tossed fireballs across their space. "This is our song, sweetie. Step aside."

Alex hesitated, but Charles made no move to stop her. The crowd already formed a wide circle in anticipation of the next show. Alex relinquished to Sharon, threw questioning eyes at Charles who looked ready to explode, and returned to the refreshment table.

"I guess she showed you," Henrietta said half jokingly. "Here, have some fruit punch so you won't choke on your pride."

Alex took the offered cup. "That was embarrassing."

Henrietta gave her an affectionate hug. "I'd like to say something really clever right now, but what I just witnessed blew everything out of my mind."

"He could have refused."

She shook her head. "They dance to certain songs, and this is one of them. I thought her red hair caught fire when he kissed you. She marched directly to the DJ and requested that song. A little early in the evening for it, but hey, what can I say! She's jealous as hell. I've never seen her act like this."

"The woman hates my guts."

"Oh, I doubt it's that serious, dear. Sharon always was a bit possessive of Charles but in a more school-chum kind of way. After all this time, it's obvious they'll never marry. Even she has to realize that."

A thought occurred to Alex. She hesitated asking. She'd already asked James, but a woman could have a different point of view. "Was Charles serious with anyone after his divorce?"

Henrietta uncovered a tray of cupcakes before answering. "He's had girlfriends, nothing I would call serious. One, however, caused quite an uproar. She disappeared and no one saw or heard from her since. The family was convinced that Charles did something with her. They hired several private detectives to snoop around but nothing ever came of it." She helped a little girl with a cup of punch. "Natalie was the woman's name. To my knowledge, they never found her. Charles sulked for months after that, hardly going out, just doing his caretaker duties and letting life pass by. We actually lost all hope that he would date anyone ever again. Then, you came along and opened up his heart. I can't tell you how happy we are to see it. I suppose that's why Sharon is overdoing the chumminess. And speaking of overdoing it..."

Alex followed Henrietta's wide eyes to the dance floor.

Whoa! It turned into a porn show! Sharon rubbed and caressed with every twist and turn in spots never to be seen in public. Her sexy moves went beyond foreplay. It went beyond dirty dancing. "Is this part of their routine?"

"No," Henrietta said with an angry glare.

Charles pushed Sharon away, but she recoiled back to his chest like a spring, determined to stay glued. He twirled her, and she recoiled again. Alex saw the anger build up in his face. Would he toss her and end it once and for all? Was Alexandra Colter brave enough to march out there and tear her hair out?

"That would create a scene," Henrietta said suddenly.

Alex peered at her with suspicion. "This mind reading of yours is starting to annoy me."

She chuckled. "You don't want to cause a stir.

Sharon has a lot of friends on this mountain. You're the newcomer."

"Point taken." Her attention went back to the dancers. "She shouldn't do that with all the children watching."

Henrietta grunted. "I don't think she gives a damn."

Charles whirled her. The dress blew upward to reveal the green panties covering a tight ass. Alex groaned. "I don't know why Charles started something with me when Sharon was still in the picture."

"Charles fell in love with you, dear. If he loved Sharon, he would have married her by now."

Or tossed her over the cliff. Alex shuddered involuntarily, unable to dismiss the thought without a chill shooting straight up her spine.

Chapter Twenty-One

Enough with the porn show. If Charles had a reasonable explanation about the exhibition dance, she would listen. It didn't mean she needed to believe it. Sharon had a thing for Charles. She won't let him go without a good fight. So it was up to him to do something about it. Whether he liked her, loved her, or detested her, Charles must be the one to put Sharon in her place. Alexandra Colter wasn't in the habit of fighting for another woman's man, and she certainly wouldn't start now.

An elderly gentleman caught her attention. She recognized him as the man on the porch at the Billings house. "Is that Billings?" she asked.

Henrietta followed her gaze. "Oh, no, that's Richard Tillerman. He's the butler at the Billings house. You already met his wife. A nice couple." She adjusted a cookie tray. "They've been with Mr. Billings for some time now. They always come to our dances. Everyone does."

"Except Billings."

Henrietta's face told her otherwise. Alex stared at her. "He's here?"

"Yes, dear, he's here." She sighed heavily. "He's a private man. When he's ready to introduce himself, he will."

Alex scanned the crowd, wondering who in the

world this man could be. "The guy's a genuine enigma. Nobody wants to talk about him. Why the big secret?"

"We are respecting his privacy, nothing more."

The music ended. The crowd applauded somewhat hesitantly at the porn show then closed the circle on the dance floor. When the next song started, Sharon clutched onto Charles. She forced him to remain on the floor.

"She's not going to let him go!" Henrietta said with surprise. "You should march over there and butt in this time. It's not one of their numbers."

Sharon had a tight grip on Charles with her face barely a paper width from his nose. His annoyed face changed to something akin to shock as Sharon whispered in his ear. Alex looked away. "As you said, Henrietta, she is not going to let him go."

"Alexandra—"

"Sharon showed her dislike of me from the beginning. She does not want me near Charles." She threw her half-full cup in the trash. "My time on this mountain is over. I'll leave by daylight."

Henrietta grabbed her arm. "You won't leave without saying goodbye to Lucy, will you?"

Alex looked around. "Where is she?"

"She got herself a boyfriend."

Alex looked at her with surprise. "Where?"

"To the right of the DJ."

Lucy sat on a chair next to a little boy. Both swung their legs freely since neither one of them could touch the floor.

"He's cute," she said and immediately felt the sadness overwhelm her. It had to end. All of it. She fell in love too quickly. She lowered her guard and let these people fill her heart with joy. She'd never get over this wonderful week. She also knew it would be impossible to say goodbye. "I'll make a quick trip to the ladies room first."

Henrietta gazed at her knowingly.

"I make no promises," Alex said.

"I'm going to kick his ass, you know that."

"You have my blessing. Tell him to finish his business with Sharon before he starts another relationship."

She nodded. "The ladies room is through the double doors and down the hall to the right. Remember, this is an elementary school. Everything is a little lower to the floor."

"Right up my alley," she said.

She couldn't feel lower than she did right now.

The bathroom was merely an excuse. Alexandra bolted straight out a side door before anyone caught her. Unfortunately, the door led to the back of the school. The parking lot was out front. As she stood debating whether to make a run for it, the same back door swung open with a bang. Two people walked out already in a heated discussion.

Charles and Sharon!

Alex crouched behind a dumpster to wait.

"What is wrong with you?" Charles argued.

"I should ask the same of you," Sharon returned. "You know your girlfriends have a tendency to disappear. Why would you think to even get involved? You can't keep this up, Charles."

"I don't want this one to disappear."

"But she will. I'm only trying to protect you from getting hurt again. And she will hurt you, Charles. You should have followed your father's advice."

"My father was an obsessive old man. He only wanted what was right for *him*."

"I wanted it. I wanted it all along. When are you going to learn that your father was right? I'm here, Charles, I will always be here. I won't disappear. I will be the one to help you get through good times and bad, and you know it. I won't disappoint you like the others. Alexandra doesn't have a clue about who and what you are."

"I like it that way."

"But you and I grew up together. There isn't anything I don't know about you." Heels scuffed on the asphalt. "You need help."

Uh-oh. Was Alexandra Colter in love with a loon? And what did Sharon and his father want? Mental help?

"I don't want you back in that gymnasium," he growled.

"While the pretty doctor is still there, you mean? Ha! She will disappear soon. Mark my words, lover boy. You invite trouble."

The door slammed. Alex heard high heels click away until they faded. She cautiously stood up. She was alone, but their words echoed in her ears. What was Charles hiding? Did he kill those two women as James suspected? The possibility was real. If he was unhinged as Sharon implicated, then yes, an attempt to leave would trigger his defenses. Was Alexandra Colter next? Was she destined to remain on the mountain in a pile of dust and bones?

She refused to wait around for the answer. She bolted toward the parking lot.

****

Alex experienced a jumbled mix of emotions as she drove back to the cabin. Up until this trip, her professional training kept her emotions in check. She had patients hang by a thread because of a lack of blood at the blood bank. She operated during power outages where even the backup generators failed. Nothing fazed her, not even a train wreck that turned her OR into a real MASH unit. Unfortunately, constantly controlling her emotions left her with the distinct inability to analyze them when they surfaced. Like now. She wasn't sure what she felt. A sense of rage perhaps combined with sadness. Heartache, yes. The end of an affair that hardly began. A lesson learned. A hard lesson without doubt. So many questions answered with the observance of one dance.

Imagine that.

Alexandra reached the dark cabin and cut the headlights. She sat there, too heartbroken to move. Tears dripped down her cheeks. She wiped them away as if she wiped something foreign off her skin. She rarely cried. Up until this vacation, she rarely experienced so many emotions. She came to this mountain to relax and forget about work. Now, she needed to return to work to forget about the mountain, to forget about the people, forget about the man who ripped her heart into shreds. Back to life in New York with its persistent loneliness, surrounded by millions of people who don't give a damn.

She stepped out of the car.

The shadow came out of nowhere. She instinctively ducked, a practiced art that went with city life. It struck the side of her head and sent her world spinning. She fell against the hood of the car when another blow connected squarely with her back. The impact forced her to her knees. Alexandra struggled to get to her feet, but the world spun too fast. She saw the pointed shoes step closer.

Fight, dammit!

Alex swung a fist at a crazed-eyed Sharon and got nothing but air. Sharon laughed harshly and readied the bat for another blow. Alex ducked. The blow missed her head by a hair and connected with her left clavicle. The bone and weapon cracked simultaneously. Alexandra screamed from the sheer intensity of the impact and hit the dirt.

"Get up!" Sharon screamed and swung her pointed shoe into Alex's back. It cut through her jacket and flesh with the ease of a dull knife. Alex screamed and tried to crawl away, but the excruciating pain left her defenseless. Sharon grabbed onto her jacket and yanked hard. She put her face close. Fire shot out of those green eyes. It was not the face of a jealous woman that Alex saw. It was the face of pure evil. The woman was unquestionably insane.

"Charles belongs to me, you Yankee Bitch! I won't let you have him!"

Alex couldn't answer. Sharon's voice rattled her eardrums as if she yelled through a megaphone.

"You are not going to marry him!" she screamed. "No one will marry him except me! Only me! Is that clear?" She shook Alex. "I let you stay on this mountain too long, you bitch! He fell in love with you, but I didn't want to kill one of our guests. That would be bad for business. His other girlfriends came from the valley so that was okay. I must eliminate all the women who come near him. All of them, do you hear me? Then he will have no choice but to marry me. Do you understand me?" She shook Alex like a rag doll. "No choice! No choice!"

Was this what Charles' father wanted? Charles and Sharon together forever? Alex damn near passed out from the pain, but Sharon's words hit like a brick. Charles had fallen in love with Alexandra. The reality of it drove Sharon completely out of her mind. She was determined to destroy her competition to force Charles into a relationship he did not want, and Alexandra Colter was next!

Sharon dragged her toward the bench.

The crazy bitch is going to throw me over!

She wouldn't let Sharon destroy her one chance at happiness. She especially wouldn't let her destroy Charles. Alex decided right then and there to stay on the mountain with him, find a way to refinance her loan, and more important, ditch the loneliness that was so much a part of her life. She wouldn't allow Sharon to take it away from her!

The badger sprang to life in a furious rage. Alex intertwined her legs with Sharon's. They hit the ground with a sprawl and a cloud of dust. Alex swung a fist and connected. She kicked, she bit, all the while struggling against Sharon's tight grip on her jacket. The woman refused to let go. The material tightened around her throat. Now struggling for air, Alex swung again and connected. Sharon screamed with rage and swung a fist at Alex's bloodied head. Alex ducked. The forward momentum slammed Sharon's fist straight into her fractured clavicle. The force jammed the bone into her lung. Her scream changed to a gasp. A fog drifted before her eyes as Sharon's lips curled into a wicked sneer.

"You're going to join Natalie at the bottom of the cliff, sweetie. I'm sure her bones are anxious for some company."

Those were the last words Alex heard before passing out.

Chapter Twenty-Two

"Are you a friggin' idiot?"

Charles whirled toward his best friend. He already received a good bashing from Henrietta. Now, James wanted to put his two cents in, and he wasn't in the mood. "Careful, pal. I won't hit a little old lady, but I might take a hefty swing at you."

"I can't believe you let her do that to you, man!"

Yes, Henrietta had said the same damn words. In her years on this mountain, he never heard such angry words out of her mouth. He ran a hand through his hair, nearly ripping it out by its roots. "I don't know what's come over Sharon. She never acted like this."

"You were never so blatantly in love either. All of us saw the change in you when Alex came onto the mountain—Sharon included. When you kissed Alex on the dance floor, I thought Sharon's red hair caught fire. And while I have your attention—" He grabbed Charles by the arm so they could stand face-to-face. "Don't you think it's odd how Sharon always showed up on your doorstep every time one of your women disappeared?"

Charles didn't like the tone of that question. He peered at his friend. "What are you saying, James?"

"Just that Sharon has an uncanny sense of timing. *You* are the one she wants, Chuckie old boy. She wants to marry you, and she won't let another woman get the chance."

Charles made a face. "She knows it will never happen." She *should* know it. He told her often enough.

"But what if her plan is to make you desperate to marry her? She knows you need to carry on the family name."

He didn't give a fig about the family name anymore. His father harped on him constantly. So much so that he married the wrong woman and made his own life miserable. Sharon was his father's choice from when they were teenagers. The old man was a friggin' fool.

"And Alex?"

His head snapped. "What about Alex? Henrietta said she went to the ladies room."

"Yeah, probably hiding with embarrassment. She's been in there long enough. I can tell you for a fact that you gave Alex every reason to pack up and leave tonight."

"No," he said with a determined shake of his head. "She knows how I feel about her."

"That was before the exhibition dance, my dumb-ass friend. Trust me, the woman was devastated."

Henrietta said the exact same words. He hurt the woman he loved. He didn't try hard enough or soon enough to pry Sharon out of his arms. He never meant to hurt Alex. He tried more not to embarrass Sharon without a thought about Alex's feelings.

Oh, God!

"I wouldn't be a bit surprised if she skipped the bathroom and went straight out the door," James continued. "She's probably halfway through Virginia by now."

Charles jerked with the words. He scanned the

crowd. "You don't think she really left, do you?"

"She doesn't owe you an explanation, chum. You're the one who needs to kiss ass to get her back."

Harry made his way through the crowd. He ran more than walked. He aimed straight for James.

"I didn't know whether to follow her or not," Harry said slightly breathless.

James gripped his arm. "When did she leave?"

"About five minutes ago."

"And Sharon?"

"Can't answer that for sure. Her car is still out front."

The exchange took Charles by surprise. He butted in. "Whoa, you two. What are you talking about?"

James studied his friend, studied him long and hard, his face full of calculation. Charles felt his nerve ends twitch. He was not staring at the face of his best friend. He was staring at the face of a trained police officer, a police officer who knew what to do with two dead bodies, a police officer who investigated arson and theft and always got results.

Finally, James stepped close to keep his voice low. "Sharon's our killer, Charles. She eliminated your girlfriends so she could have free reign with you. I just can't prove it."

He stood back, aghast. "Then how do you know it's her?"

Harry spoke. "I was heading to Zach Stewart's place when I met Alex on the road. We talked for a while before Zach called to remind me to get my ass moving. While I worked on his Chevy, I saw Sharon drive by. Then almost as quickly, she headed back down. I thought that was odd until I heard the tires squeal. I knew Alex was on the road so I high-tailed it down. She was okay, shaken but angry. I reported it to James. I offered to drive her back to the cabin, but she refused. After she went into the woods, I took a walk further down to the next curve. I saw Sharon waiting. When she saw me, she took off."

Charles peered at the two men. "Are you saying Sharon attempted to run over Alex?"

James answered. "Sharon told me she lost traction around the curve. She also said she waited around the curve to apologize to Alex. But Sharon was already on my radar." He touched his friend's arm. "I'm sorry, chum. I hadn't ruled you out as a suspect. It was still possible that you and Sharon acted together so I enlisted Harry's help to keep an eye on Alex. I kept my eye on Sharon. Between the two of us, we always knew where the other one was. Then I overheard you and Sharon arguing outside the general store. She wanted you to get rid of Alex's photo in your phone. Remember? It was your answer and Sharon's reaction that finally convinced me she acted alone."

Charles jerked. "I told her it was time to get a life of her own."

"Right. Then I witnessed the interaction of Sharon and Alex as Alex approached with Lucy. Alex's face said it all, chum. She looked frightened. I don't know what Sharon said to her, but it was enough to put fear in her face. That convinced me Sharon was our murderer, that she acted alone, yet I still couldn't prove it."

"Did Alex know it was Sharon?"

He shook his head. "She may have suspected you, chum, if Sharon put ideas into her head."

The two men locked eyes. Silent words passed

between them. Charles turned sharply, took out his phone and hit the speed dial. He paced while listening. The pacing increased with each ring. Anger turned to fury. "She's not answering. She may not want to talk to me."

"Either way, I need to know where she is," James said. "Go up to the cabin. If she's there, call me. Harry and I will start searching for Sharon. We'll start here, but she knows this mountain as well as the rest of us."

All three men took off in different directions.

****

The Red Baron skidded to a stop at Rosebay cabin. Charles stepped out of the cab and was on the porch before the dust settled. Darkness surrounded him. Not a sign of life or lights anywhere. No car either. Did she pack up and leave already?

"I'll kill Sharon," he vowed.

James was right. It took a lot of soul searching, but the truth stared him in the face. Ever since his divorce, he had difficulty maintaining a relationship with a woman. He never understood why. They would suddenly call it off without explanation, always a brief note to say good-bye. He would never hear from them again. And yes, Sharon always came by to offer condolences. He never understood how she knew that another woman dumped him. He attributed it to a women's six sense, the one that always saw through a man's tough façade no matter how much he pretended not to care. They usually wound up in bed doing the physical need shit that he hated so much. Absolutely no love involved. He put a stop to their repeated liaisons after the last woman mysteriously left. He finally decided to forget about a family life and concentrate instead on the mountain.

Then Alexandra came along. When he saw her standing by the car, his heart stopped. She was so petite with a voice that threw him into sensory overload. After she collided into his back, she looked awkward and shy and just...absolutely adorable. He nearly melted right in front of her. From that moment, he could not shake the exhilarating feeling whenever she stood near, but he remained cautious. He never understood why his relationships ended so abruptly.

Now, he understood.

The first body they found was Gloria. He had only gone with her several weeks when he received her goodbye note. They identified the body from the necklace he gave her. Dental records confirmed it. When Alex found the scarf on the trail, he ran straight to James with it. He had bought the scarf for Sheryl while they shopped in the valley. But the one whose family caused such a stink was Natalie. They had yet to find her. She was on this mountain somewhere, of that he was certain.

Charles fumbled with his key ring when his shoulder brushed against the door. It opened with a faint creak. He stepped in and slammed on the lights.

The cabin was deserted. The bedroom closet stood open and bare. The stove was cold, the bed untouched. He jerked open one dresser drawer after another, all bare. No suitcase. No nothing. In the bathroom, a damp towel hung on a rack, but that could be from a shower before the dance.

He hurried to the kitchen. She left food in the refrigerator. Understandable. The roses were dumped in the trash. Understandable there, too. She must hate him.

The key to the cabin lay on the counter. He stared at it, remembering the day he handed it to her. He marveled at the small hand that took the key.

His heart sank. She was gone. She left without saying goodbye. He took out his phone and again tried her number.

His head snapped toward the open door.

The ring came from outside!

He ran out, following the rings. Then he stopped dead. *The phone was under the porch*?

Charles grabbed the flashlight from his truck and dropped to all four's. He swept the beam under the floorboards. Her cell phone was there, about a foot in, ringing away. He stood to his feet and stared at his name on the caller ID. Then a thought struck him. He ran back to the kitchen and yanked open that one special cabinet.

Her purse and medical bag sat on the shelf.

Out of sight, out of mind.

A woman would not pack all her belongings and leave her purse. A doctor would never leave a medical bag. And now her phone. She could have dropped the phone on the way out of the cabin, but nothing explained her purse and medical bag.

Sharon!

Charles rushed outside again and swept the flashlight beam across the ground not really certain what he looked for...until he found it. There were distinct signs of a struggle in the dirt. Two different sets of shoe prints: one high heels, the other sneakers. He also found drag marks that ended abruptly near a set of small tires. Then he found a splintered baseball bat hidden in a bush. Several bloodstains covered one end.

The coroner said the weapon was probably a baseball bat.

Dear Lord, no!

Panic turned to terror. Shaking uncontrollably, he activated his phone when it suddenly rang in his hand.

He nearly jumped out of his skin.

It was James. "Charles, I'm about a mile south of the general store, near Jenkins' place. You better get down here."

"Did you find Sharon?"

"Yes, she's here with me."

"How about Alex?"

Silence. "Get down here, Charles."

The Red Baron wouldn't fly fast enough.

Chapter Twenty-Three

Charles saw the bright orange glow as he rounded a bend. Flames shot upward on the side of the mountain burning wildly through brush and trees. A fire. Like he gave a shit about a fire. The whole goddamned forest could burn for all he cared.

The Red Baron skidded to a stop just as the wail of fire sirens hit his ears. A crowd had gathered by the cliff side, all eyes staring downward toward the flames. He ran to James who stood off to the side. The orange glow reflected off a face full of despair.

It was the Yugo. Flames rose from within it, scorching every thing within reach about a hundred feet down the mountain.

Charles let out a cry and started down. He blindly fought the men trying to hold him back.

"No, Charles, it's too late!"

Even with all his fury, common sense told him it was too late. But he had to know. He struggled. "Let go!"

"We don't know if she's in there." James stepped into his path. "The flames were too intense when I arrived. Charles." He grabbed hold of his friend's arm. "When we separated at the school, I got a call about this car fire. At first, I thought she lost control on the curve, but I see no evidence of that on the road." His grip tightened. "Sharon was jumping all over the road when

219

I got here. It looked like some sort of ritual dance. She smells of gas, and she's covered with blood. She also looks like she took a good beating."

Charles' eyes, riveted on the flames, snapped to James' face as the words set in. "Where is she?"

Charles saw her before James answered. Three men couldn't hold him back. He glared at all of them, James included, and held a finger up in warning. "No!" He marched to Sharon.

Sharon stood happily by the patrol car, her green eyes sparkling with glee while staring down at the flames. Blood stained the point of her shoe. More blood smeared the front of her green dress along with smudges of dirt. Several bruises dotted her face. And yes, she smelled of gasoline. He grabbed her roughly by the arm. "Did you do this?"

"Charles, dear, how nice to see you. Did you bring the marshmallows?"

He nearly swung at her with a closed fist. "Did you do this, Sharon?" He shook her. "Answer me!"

"Don't be so rough. I warned her about these treacherous roads. She obviously didn't want to listen. So, it's just me again, lover boy. Just you and me, like always, like it should be. You can't deny our destiny."

James stepped between them. A timely maneuver. Charles was about to grab her long slender neck and choke her to death.

Destiny indeed. Charles shot him a black look but turned rapidly away.

He felt sick as he watched the firefighters fight the flames. His chest had an empty hole where his heart used to be. The one woman he wanted so badly, the one woman who made everything feel so right was gone forever. All these years, Sharon denied him a family life. She denied him love and above all denied his legacy. There remained a shell of a man just like the big black shell of metal stuck against a clump of burnt mountain bushes.

Henrietta made her way through the crowd to stand beside him. Tears flowed freely down her cheeks smudging what little make-up she wore.

"Alex told me Sharon wanted her off this mountain," he said half choking on the words. "I told her we were old friends."

She patted his arm. "Don't blame yourself. I didn't listen either. I have a strange feeling Sharon made her intentions well known before Alexandra said anything to us."

The day of her hike for one. She took a spill. She never elaborated nor did he ask. He simply picked the pine needles out of her silky hair. "James is right," he mumbled. "I'm a friggin' idiot. I'm never going to forgive myself."

Henrietta put her head against his arm, too overwhelmed with emotions to speak.

A firefighter walked over and asked them to step to the side. Harry's tow truck inched its way toward the cliff edge. The fire was out, the smoke cleared. It was time to retrieve the car. A firefighter grabbed the hook from Harry's truck, and with Harry working a lever, the firefighter slowly descended the incline. Charles watched with a helplessness he never experienced. He usually gave the orders. He always knew the course of action. The take-charge man on the mountain. Now, he couldn't even think. He watched as the firefighter wrapped the hook somewhere on the underbelly of the car. Within twenty minutes, the burned-out Yugo scraped its way uphill. No one said a word—except Sharon who giggled gleefully.

With the car safely positioned on the asphalt, James looked at Charles. Charles looked at James. Both men approached the car with trepidation, flashlights ready. Neither wanted to find what they were looking for.

They didn't. Charles' heart skipped a few beats when he saw no evidence of a body within the car. The two men exchanged glances in silence. James grabbed a crowbar from the tow truck and pried the hatchback. A smoldering suitcase released a puff of smoke as the hatch opened. Charred clothes, Alex's hiking boots, the remains of a backpack, all reduced to ashes. And no body. *She isn't in the car!*

James directed his flashlight downhill.

Charles copied him. "Do you think she fell out?" An edge of hope came with the words.

"It's possible, but there's no place for her to roll. The brush is too thick."

Charles turned to the firefighters. "Let's get the floodlights down there! I don't give a damn if every bush and tree is uprooted. Search the hillside!"

The entire mountainside lit up like daytime. Four firefighters descended for a search, Charles and James among them.

An agonizing forty minutes passed as they searched further and further down the mountain. "We should have found her by now," he said.

"Unless she wasn't in the car at all," James answered. "Sharon could have tossed her out anywhere between here and the cabin."

Their eyes locked. Charles felt his blood boil in his veins. The rage, the anguish at one woman wrenched his gut. Sharon interfered in his life one too many times. She became just like his overbearing father, always trying to control every aspect of his life. Well, not anymore, dammit! The one woman he wanted in his life was not with him, and come hell or high water, he would find her. He scurried up the hill and ran to Sharon. He grabbed her arm. She winced from the pressure. "Where is she?"

"You're hurting me!"

"I'm about to do some serious damage to you if you don't answer me."

"I have nothing to say."

"Answer me!" He nearly ripped her arm right out of its socket. "Answer me!"

Her face turned to him with a sweet smile. Her eyes, however, were unfocused. "Charles, dear, we left the dance too early. Nobody saw our closing number."

He shook her. "What did you do with Alex?"

She grew thoughtful. "We don't have an Alex on the mountain. An Adrian and an Andrew, but no Alex. Is he new at the school?"

He stepped back and ran both hands through his hair. Anger filled him. Hatred even. But the woman was unquestionably insane. He struggled to control what boiled inside him. His urgency to find Alex was paramount, but rage needed to be suppressed. Could he pry the information out of her? What would Alex do? She had a way with people. What was her key?

Openness. Without doubt, an openness that made everyone comfortable. Forcing his emotions aside, he took several deep breaths then turned back to Sharon.

He slipped his arm over her shoulder. "Let's take a walk."

"You hurt my arm!"

"I'll make up for it later. We always do." He hit a nerve with those words, and she relaxed. He guided her to the opposite side of the road.

"We put on quite a show tonight, didn't we?" he began.

"Yes, we did. We should be a professional dance team. I don't know why you object so much. I hope I erased all thoughts of you teaching that doctor how to dance. She's hopeless."

Something popped inside him. He fought to control it. His hand was too close to her slender neck. "Do you think she will show up at the next dance?"

"She will never show her face on this mountain again. I guarantee it." She wrapped her arm around his waist. "I took care of her for you, Charles dear."

"I'm not so sure about that, Sharon. She might have fallen out of the car."

"She was never in the car."

He patted her arm, resisting the urge to break it in two. "Clever girl. I hope you dumped her in a safe spot."

"They will never find her."

"We never found Natalie either. Where is she?"

"Worm bait."

Every second that ticked by meant a life slowly drifting away. Alex's life. He closed his eyes and silently prayed for help. "Is Alexandra dead?"

"Oh, yes. She was dead when I tossed her."

The rage reached a full boil. His childhood friend turned into a vicious serial killer, the same girl he played hide and seek with, the woman who let him explore his masculinity while she explored her femininity. His father pressured them to marry. The old man should be turning over in his grave right about now.

He swallowed his rage. And more. He fought back tears!

Charles cleared his throat. "I hope she isn't where a guest can find her. You know how much the income from these cabins mean to the folks up here. You killed a guest this time, dear."

"Yes. I didn't want to, but she wouldn't heed my warnings. She didn't stay away from you, Charles."

That was because he couldn't stay away from her.

"I think it's high time you stopped with this caretaker charade," she snapped. "I refuse to be the caretaker's wife."

"Yes," he said with great control, "it's time for everything to stop. Where is Alexandra?"

"Forget her, Charles. She's dead."

"She's got a lot of family who will come looking, Sharon. You know how Natalie's family caused a ruckus. The same will happen with Alexandra's. They might lock me away this time. You don't want that, do you?" He let the words sink in. "We could bury her together."

Sharon's wild-eyed face grew thoughtful. "You'll never reach her. She's at the bottom of the mountain."

"Back at Rosebay?"

"Yes, a straight drop down."

Charles wondered how long a prison sentence he'd get as his fingers slipped tightly around her throat.

Chapter Twenty-Four

So cold. So very cold.

A swift breeze blew from below. It penetrated her jacket and hit the warm blood from her wounds. It sent a violent shiver through her veins, forcing her into the world of the living.

Alexandra opened her eyes.

A familiar view came into focus: the nightlights of Roanoke. The clouds of earlier moved off, leaving only a few strays floating. Bright stars twinkled here and there to say hello. A sliver of a moon struggled to outshine them. An elegant white curve in a dark sky. It did little to help her see.

She had no idea where she was. She felt around. Pain shot out in all directions with the slightest movement. Her clavicle, her ass, her back, her head. Warm blood everywhere. Her fingers were stuck together from dried blood. Not a pleasant feeling. She forced them apart and took a good look around.

Alex was sprawled out on a nest of some sort. Presumably, Sharon tossed her off the cliff, and she had landed on the young pine trees jutting from the cliff crevices. She saw the cliff wall above easily enough. Below, she saw nothing but a black void.

Broken branches jabbed her back and butt. Any shift to alleviate the pressure created a series of snaps in response. At one point, her body jerked downward and stopped. Scared the shit out of her. She felt around for something to hang onto should her nest give way, but other than a tree trunk, there was nothing. Just as well. She had only one arm to use. The other was immobile because of the broken clavicle. Her breath came out in puffs from a collapsed lung. Labored breathing. The body's struggle to suck in much needed oxygen. Her teeth chattered like an antique typewriter. She tried controlling it, but it vibrated every cell in her body. Shock was inevitable. From blood loss. From trauma. From cold. She felt alone, abandoned, and could state with complete honesty that she felt like crap.

Alex searched in her pockets for her cell phone. Gone. Probably at the bottom of the mountain.

That damn redhead. No one would know that she left the dance to lurk in the shadows by the cabin. No one would know that Alexandra Colter dangled on some tree branches off the cliff still alive, struggling to breathe. No one would know a damn thing. She was destined to die as she lived her life: alone. *I don't want to be alone anymore, dammit*! She never realized how much she hated the loneliness until she came onto the mountain. She hated it even more now perched on a nest away from those who cared.

"Help!"

She tried anyway, but her lungs held insufficient volume to power her voice. It took all she had to shout that one word.

In time, the shivering subsided. Death wasn't far, she knew. She accepted the hand dealt her with one misgiving: she failed to prevent Sharon from ruining Charles' life. He deserved happiness. He deserved a wife and loving family, not a trail of bodies because of an obsessive woman.

She drifted in and out of a sleep-like state, her senses dulled by the shock. She did smell pine, however. Charles smelled like pine. It flowed out of his pores and intoxicated her senses while they slept. She sucked it in then; she sucked it in now. At least she would die with the memory of a wonderful night spent with a wonderful man.

She slept.

"Alex!"

She jerked awake, not sure if she really heard her name or whether it was part of a dream.

"Alex! Alex!"

Several people called her name.

"Down here!" It came out as a squeak.

"Alex!"

Flashlights swung in every direction, none of them her way. She lifted her good arm hoping someone would catch the movement.

"Alex!"

That voice was louder and stronger, coming directly above. She recognized it immediately. Tears streamed down her cheeks because he would never hear her. "Charles."

The beam swung in her direction. She instinctively shut her eyes to shield against the brightness.

"Don't move, sweetheart! I'm coming down!"

A lot of movement and yelling came from above. Then bright lights lowered on both sides to illuminate the cliff wall. She saw with a start that she fell at least 200 feet!

"I'm coming!"

He didn't have to announce it. Dirt and stones

preceded him. She used her good arm to cover her face.

"I'm here," he said.

Charles dangled from a metal cable right by her head. A flood of relief swept through her at the sight of him. She was too weak to feel anything else, but one very distinctive feeling surfaced. She knew he would come looking for her. Because he cared. Because he loved her. The one man who made the loneliness disappear. Alex met his eyes, so full of concern—and fear.

"Nice of you...to drop by. Sharon."

"Yes, I know what happened." His face changed to granite. "I'm putting this cervical collar on you."

His voice had the authoritative edge that she recognized. She struggled to focus on his face.

"We won't be able to lower a basket to lift you out. I will not be able to stabilize any of your injuries. Do you understand?"

She nodded. In other words, prepare for pain. No way to use a backboard or basket. Time wasn't on her side with a precarious nest about to give. She stopped him from putting on the collar.

"It's necessary," he insisted.

"I need...to tell you...that Sharon fractured...my left collarbone. That bone went...into my lung. I'm convinced...I do not have...a spinal jury. If I'm wrong, I will...deal with the consequences."

"*We* will deal with the consequences," he said through tight teeth. "Listen to me carefully. You're to lean forward and wrap your good arm around my neck. At the same time, I will slip my arm under your butt. We will not waste time or movement. I want it done in one sweep. You are not to release your arm from around my neck until we reach the top of the cliff. Is that clear?"

"Yes, sir." For once, she appreciated his drill sergeant tone.

"I'll count to three. On three, I want you to move." His face lost some of the granite. It did not lose the fear. "You can do this, Alex. If there was ever a time to gather your strength, this is it. On three, move. One, two, *three*!"

Her arm went up. His arm slipped under her ass. He lifted and pressed her to his chest as her nest crackled and snapped before falling into the void. The crowd above cheered. They hung freely for several long seconds, dangling from the thick metal cable. His arm held her tight while his heat radiated through her clothes to thaw her frozen skin. His arm felt so good she bore the excruciating pain in silence. She put her head on his shoulder.

"I'm so sorry," he whispered.

That did it. The tears poured out of her eyes in buckets. Every emotion surfaced, and she fought back none of them.

The crowd cheered again as they reached the top. Hands grabbed her. Charles relayed her injuries to the ambulance crew as they lifted her from his arm. Then came the comfort of a stretcher. Someone slipped an oxygen mask on her face. Someone else used a scissors to cut off her sleeve. A paramedic started an IV line. All this so quickly, so fast, she saw only a blur. She motioned for James to come over. He put his face close to hear.

"Natalie is down there," she whispered.

He said nothing, merely kissed her forehead in

answer. She decided it was a good time to drift off to sleep. She searched the many faces for the one she wanted. He stood separated from the crowd. He had his face buried in his hands while kneeling by the Red Baron.

The big man shook from uncontrollable sobs.

Chapter Twenty-Five

Alexandra woke in a hospital bed. A strange feeling of *Welcome to My World* passed through her groggy brain since she lived the last seven years buried deep inside hospital walls. It was a private room and large, decorated in soothing colors of mauve and pale lavender.

Lucy's red Elmo doll stared back from the foot of the bed looking as nonchalant as usual. Tears formed in her eyes. They were happy tears because of a bunch of wonderful people who embraced her from the moment she set foot on the mountain. She wanted to hold onto that feeling. She wanted to be part of the love they so easily shared, to be a part of their community and to forever discard the loneliness that was so much a part of her existence.

If only she could make it work.

Familiar apparatus surrounded her bed. An IV pole on the right dangled two bags of fluid. Both connected to her right wrist via long clear tubing. She inspected the needle site out of habit. A monitor on the wall showed a good heart rate and blood pressure. Acceptable doctor numbers. Her brain overflowed with questions, the "where was I", "how was I doing" questions. No one was nearby to answer them.

Five bouquets of flowers sat on a wheeled display cart. They scented the entire room.

"The flowers are pretty, aren't they, Elmo?"

He would appreciate them. He was red just like the large bouquet of red roses on the top shelf of the cart.

Her left arm rested in a sling. She wiggled her fingers just to be sure she could. She lifted the sheets to check her legs. She wiggled her toes down there, too. A chest tube stuck out of her left side. Inevitable. The damn thing pinched.

A tall, distinguished woman wandered into the room looking thoughtful and preoccupied. She wore an exquisitely tailored business suit that fit a mature figure. She was in her mid-fifties at a guess with a stethoscope draped around her neck. Alexandra wondered if she wandered into the wrong room since her mind seemed so far away. In answer to the thought, the woman suddenly looked up to see Alexandra looking back at her.

"Dr. Colter! I'm glad you're awake. I'm Dr. Eileen Tagleone. Mr. Billings asked me to personally attend to you." She stopped and sniffed. "It smells like a flower shop in here." She extended her hand.

"Nice to meet you." Alexandra gave her a limp handshake.

"Let me check your lungs before I sit for a little chit-chat." She did. Then she pulled up a chair alongside the bed and sat down.

"How long have I been out?"

"Off and on for two days. I expect you want to know about your injuries. I managed to put your clavicle back together without the use of pins. It looks remarkably well on X-ray. Your pneumothorax was at 45% when you arrived. That, too, is rapidly improving. I put twelve stitches on the side of your head and eight stitches on your back. You sustained a moderate concussion, two fractured ribs, numerous cuts and abrasions, but no spinal injuries. I had you X-rayed from head to toe when you arrived. Your blood loss was moderate. Your hemoglobin stayed within our accepted parameters. Overall, you survived an ordeal that should have killed you. You are one damn lucky woman."

Alex smiled weakly. "Forgive me if I don't feel lucky."

Dr. Tagleone gave her a warm smile. "I understand. However, you are doing well. I have ordered a normal diet for you. I'd like to see you eat all of it since you're such a small thing. You will be with us for a while so if you need anything, just ask. From a financial standpoint, Harlan is taking care of everything."

Alex looked at her, puzzled. "Who's Harlan?"

"Harlan Billings. He has been our hospital benefactor for many years, ever since his mother died. So naturally, when he asked me to oversee your care, there was no question about it. He feels responsible since one of his residents attacked you. I gather you are a guest on the mountain?"

"Yes."

"Do you have anyone we should notify?"

Alex shook her head. Not a damn soul.

Dr. Tagleone's shrewd hazel eyes studied her. "You *are* Alexandra Colter from New York, correct?"

That surprised her. She studied the woman. "Have we met?"

"Not really but I know you. I attended your lecture on laparoscopic resection at Columbia. I happened to be

234

in New York for a conference when a colleague suggested we attend. You have quite a reputation in New York. Do you have any plans to relocate?"

"At the moment, I have no idea what I'm doing."

"That's understandable." She stood to her feet and replaced the chair back against the wall. "I'll be checking on your progress every day. X-rays daily to follow the resolution of your pheumo. Any pain?"

"It's tolerable."

"Medication is ordered if you need it. Don't be bashful." She extended her hand. "It's nice to meet you, Dr. Colter. I'm going to give you something to think about while you're convalescing. The head of our surgical residency program is retiring. I've been specifically looking for a younger surgeon skilled in the latest techniques. I already checked your credentials, and I'm more than impressed with your reputation. If you feel like coming down here to stay, perhaps you might consider the position. You'd be an excellent asset to the hospital."

A teaching position. Was she kidding? "I'm flattered." Surprised. Shocked. Thrilled. "I don't know what to say."

"Don't say anything. Just think about it."

"Are you head of staff?"

"No, no. I'm the CEO. I'll see you tomorrow." She turned to leave.

"Dr. Tagleone?"

She turned back. "Yes?"

"Has—uh…anyone been here to see me?"

Her mouth spread into that warm smile again. "I assume you are referring to the dark-haired man who hasn't left this hospital since you arrived."

Alexandra smiled back at her. "Yes."

"I forced him to go downstairs to get something to eat. I'm sure he won't be long. He'll wolf down a burger in ten seconds flat. I just pray he doesn't choke to death."

She left the room.

A teaching position. Her dream job. Still unobtainable because of heavy debts. All the way down here in—eh...where the hell was she? She forgot to ask.

A large Styrofoam cup with a straw sat on the bed table to the right. Naturally, the table was pushed far beyond reach. She tried anyway.

"I'll get it."

Charles came out of nowhere and grabbed the cup. He put the straw to her lips. The water tasted wonderful, and she sucked in half the liquid without stopping. Afterwards, he watched her. She watched him back. Neither of them spoke. If words were to be spoken, they had to come from him first.

"How do you feel?" he asked.

"Okay." A bold lie. She probably looked as bad as she felt.

He stared at her for the longest time. His face was a mask of anxiety and nervousness, both well-deserved emotions. He also looked uncomfortable. Finally, he cleared his throat.

"I need to explain a few things."

He strolled to the window and stared out. "Sharon and I grew up together. You already know that. We never had anything that resembled a relationship. I had no feelings toward her except those of a friend." He gave her a quick sideward glance. "She was there as...huh—"

"Physical need shit."

"Yes, that physical need shit." He said it sadly, without looking at her. "That's why I said what I did to you. I've had enough of sex without love." He paused.

She remained silent; he was on his own here.

"Looking back, I realize how influential Sharon was in all my relationships, even my marriage. She kept herself on the good side of my father, and he in turn stayed angry with me for not marrying Sharon. I went through a holy hell with my ex-wife and blamed the whole thing on my father. None of it on Sharon." He paused again, clearly struggling for words. He stared with unseeing eyes out the window.

"I seldom dated after my divorce. When I did, the relationship never lasted. Sharon always dropped by when they ended. I was too stupid to realize that *she* was the reason they ended. Her obsession led to murder. She assumed that I would marry her if I wanted a family life. She assumed wrong, of course. I would rather stay single than to be stuck in a relationship with a woman I didn't love. I had already accepted my single life and the disappointment of not carrying on the family name when you came along."

He turned toward the bed. He did not approach. Instead, he stood with his back to the window looking at her. His gaze was full of uncertainty.

"When I rounded the corner of the cabin that day to see you standing by your car, I never in my life melted on the spot just by looking at a woman. Everyone saw the change in me. I walked on air. I floated even higher every time I answered my phone because there you were, asleep on the hammock like a gorgeous sleeping beauty. I fell terribly in love, but I kept it cool. I never understood why all my girlfriends disappeared without explanation. I received curt little notes telling me it was over. It never dawned on me that they were written by the same hand—Sharon's."

"So that's why you made me promise to tell you before I left the mountain," she said. "I thought it was a strange request."

He nodded and took a few steps away from the window. "Not long after I shot the photo, Sharon borrowed my phone to make a call. I never registered the change in her when she saw it. I remember she gave me a severe look. I dismissed it without thought." He paused to meet her eyes. "Harry told me what happened on the road."

At least now he knew. "She tried to make me a hood ornament."

His face twitched. "Why didn't you say something?"

"You wouldn't have believed me. It was her word against mine."

He thought about that comment. "You're right. I still can't believe what she's done." He clenched his jaw. "I've been so blind. When we found out you weren't in the car—"

Alex started. "What car?"

He stared. Then realization struck. "That's right. You have no idea what happened. Sharon packed all your clothes into the Yugo and drove it over a cliff. She wanted to make it look like you were leaving the mountain but had an accident along the way. It was her tough luck that the car's light weight prevented it from barreling down the mountainside. She gave it a good dousing of gas so nothing was salvageable." He rubbed the back of his neck while staring down at the floor. "My whole world stopped spinning because we thought you were still inside."

"She burned up my car?"

"That, and all your clothes. I'm sorry."

Alex groaned.

"Better the car than you," he said softly.

He turned abruptly back toward the window. It was an obvious attempt to hide his face, but he could not disguise the catch in his voice. Nor will he erase her memory of a proud man brought to his knees while sobbing like a baby. The image would remain with her forever.

"What happened to Sharon?"

He didn't answer right away, nor did she repeat the question. She let him take his time. She wasn't going anywhere.

Charles finally turned with eyes moist and red. A profound sadness covered his face. "We had to lock her away. She went completely off her nut when she discovered everyone rushing to Rosebay to find you. I never felt such an outpouring of love as I have that night, Alex. Everyone came with one purpose in mind: to help me find the woman I fell in love with."

Charles grabbed the chair by the wall and placed it on the right side of her bed. He sat down and took her hand in both of his. He held it gently, like fragile glass. She felt like fragile glass, all patched up and glued back together. "James filed murder charges against Sharon, but it became clear she needed to be institutionalized. He used every restraint he carried just to control her." He toyed with her fingers, moving them one by one. Cuts and bruises covered her skin.

"Harry loved Sharon very much," he continued. "It was a relationship that never went anywhere. He was too short for her, and worse, he couldn't dance. She passed up a good man for one who had absolutely no interest."

"Harry might resent you."

He shook his head. "He's a sensible man with a good head on his shoulders. He knew he fought a losing battle. Some years ago, we discussed teaching him to dance, but he could never do anything about his height. He tried lifts, but Sharon was just too tall."

"I'm more Harry's size."

"Yes, and I was very surprised he didn't challenge me."

"Why, because he saw me first?" She cocked her head while meeting his gaze. "You don't strike me as a man to be challenged. You have this air about you; I really can't put my finger on it. It's unusual to see for a—"

"Caretaker?"

She sighed. "Yes, a caretaker. I didn't mean to insult you."

"You're not." He kissed her hand. "I'm so sorry this happened, Alexandra."

"Me, too. Now I have to go shopping for a new car."

He smiled slightly, but his eyes remained sad. "There's one more thing I want to talk about." He looked at her squarely. "The dance."

Great. Like she needed to be reminded.

"I hurt you, and I haven't stopped kicking myself."

She took her hand out of his. "Sharon should have let me be. If she hadn't attacked me, I'd have been halfway back to New York before the dance was over."

He sat back and stared. "Seriously?"

"Yes, I was defeated. Sharon made her intentions clear on several occasions. The fact that you didn't push her away on the dance floor convinced me that I had been a fool."

"I take full responsibility for not stopping her. You aren't saying anything I haven't heard from James and Henrietta. The truth is I told Sharon it was our last dance. She became furious and latched onto me while saying things I don't care to repeat. She became much worse after I told her I had a new partner to teach."

"Who?"

"You. If you can forgive me. Sharon went ballistic. It didn't help when I told her you were going to be my wife. I think that more than anything put her over the edge. What?"

She stared, wide-eyed. "I never agreed to marry you. We have obstacles to discuss, and trust me, Charles, there are plenty. But not today. This chest tube hurts like hell." She shifted, felt the tube pull, and winced. "Now I know what I put my patients through when I insert one of these damn things. No, I'm serious, Charles. We won't discuss anything today. I want you to go home and rest. You look tired. Don't come back for a few days."

"I'm not sure I want to listen."

"You have to. Otherwise, I inform the nursing staff to restrict your visits."

His eyebrows arched. "You'd do that?"

"Yes. Just leave me alone for a few days and let me think. I'll call you when I'm ready."

He stood to his feet with a frown crinkling into his

forehead. "All right, I'll go. Harry is taking care of the cabins so I'll relieve him." He put the chair back against the wall. "Is there anything I can do before I leave?"

"Yes. Tell me where I am."

He started. Then he relaxed with a soft chuckle. "Yeah, I guess you wouldn't know. We airlifted you from the mountain to one of the best hospitals in Roanoke. They wouldn't let me on the helicopter so James drove me here with full lights and sirens running."

"How will you get back?"

"I've made arrangements. Anything else?"

"There is one thing." She studied him. "I need to be reminded of what Sharon tried to destroy."

Without hesitation, his lips came down to meet hers. His lips were full of love. The man loved her. She felt it, had felt it from the very beginning. Her big problem was all the questions rolling around inside her head. When their lips parted, a mist clouded his eyes.

"I'll do anything you ask," he whispered and left the room.

Chapter Twenty-Six

They were her terms and he agreed to them, but by the second day, she missed him terribly. She wondered if she would. Her life changed so drastically since her arrival on the mountain all because of him. He was there every single day, filling her heart with a joy she never knew she lacked. Still, doubts lingered about their relationship. She and Charles lived in two different worlds: she, a big city surgeon working in a big city hospital making good money; he, a caretaker on the mountain attending seven tourist cabins. She knew nothing more about him, his family, his education, his paycheck. She only knew she loved him. That was a certainty that surprised even her.

Love won't pay the bills, however.

"Dr. Colter, you're looking all down in the dumps."

It was her nurse, Nadine. She walked into the room with several bags of IV fluid. "How come I haven't seen your man around here?"

"I told him to stay away."

"That handsome dude? Honey, you need your head examined. You want me to put in a psych consult for you?"

Alexandra chuckled. "It might not be a bad idea."

Nadine hung an antibiotic bag and attached it to the IV line. As she programmed the drip time in the machine, she said, "Anything you want to talk about? Sometimes it helps to talk out loud about a problem. I tell my kids that all the time."

"Thank you, Nadine, but I'm too confused to put anything into words."

She finished with the IV and turned a kind face toward her. "My momma always told me never to make an important decision when I was tired. I found that to be a good piece of advice."

Sound wisdom. Despite everything that happened, she was very much in love with Charles. She wanted to be with him forever but could not decide what to do with her career. Marrying him meant living in Virginia, specifically Billings Mountain. The money to help pay off her loan was in big city hospitals. She asked him to stay away so she could think. Well, she couldn't think, dammit, because he wasn't here! She had so many questions and made no progress whatsoever.

Visitors arrived the next day. James, Lucy, and Henrietta came bobbing through the door full of smiles. James carried a fruit basket. Lucy carried wildflowers, which she promptly handed over. Henrietta carried a shopping bag. Their friendly faces lifted her spirits to soaring.

"Thought you might like some company," Henrietta said.

Lucy stepped in with a huff. "I want a hug!"

"You wait your turn." Henrietta leaned over and kissed Alexandra on the forehead. Then she took the wildflowers and went in search of a vase. In a hospital, that meant a cup.

James also leaned down for a kiss. His kiss was a little more personal. He pulled away with sparkling eyes. "I can't do that once you get married. You-know-who will kill me."

"What about me?" Lucy asked with a great deal of indignation.

"If you promise to be careful, I'll let James help you up onto my bed," Alex said.

"Really? All right, I promise."

James lifted her and placed her carefully on the right side of the bed. Alex gave Lucy a one-armed hug and kissed her. "Elmo has been keeping me company."

"That was his job."

"Did you miss him?"

"I missed you more."

My God! That comment shot straight to her heart!

"How do you feel?" Henrietta asked, returning.

"Better since the three of you came through the door. I can't believe how much I've missed everyone."

"We missed you, too. That's why we took such a long ride. We'll make a day of it while we're here."

"We're gonna have pizza!" Lucy stated.

"Yum, my favorite food."

"I bought you clothes," Henrietta continued. She held up the shopping bag. "Yours were ruined and, of course, Sharon destroyed the rest. Nothing fancy. Jeans and sweatshirt. It will get you out of here so you won't have to wear a hospital gown."

"Thanks, Henrietta. You can put it on my charge slip."

"No need, honey. Charles paid. He gave me all the sizes before they tossed everything in the trash, sneakers included. I didn't bring your purse though."

Alex looked at her. "My purse?"

James answered. "Sharon didn't know you kept the

purse and medical bag in the kitchen. She grabbed what she saw and tossed everything in the car."

"When you coming home?" Lucy asked.

Tears welled up in her eyes with that question. She hid them from Lucy by kissing her hair. She couldn't hide them from James or Henrietta. "Oh, they'll release me eventually. In the meantime, I have to be a good little girl and follow orders."

"You're the doc-torr. You should be giving the orders."

"I'm a recuperating doc-torr," she countered.

"Why don't you and Lucy take a trip upstairs," Henrietta said to James. "It will give Alexandra and me a chance to talk."

James agreed. He reached to grab Lucy. "All right, squirt. Give Alex a big kiss. We'll go say hello to everybody upstairs." James lifted Lucy out of the bed and leaned down for his turn. "Gad, you are gorgeous even all banged up. I am so jealous. If you ever change your mind—"

"He will break you in two," Henrietta said.

"What's upstairs?" Alex asked.

"Pediatrics. Lucy was here for several months." Henrietta turned to them. "Yes, go show the nurses how big you got. I'll meet the two of you down in the lobby. Oh, and James, say hello to Caroline for me."

He wiggled his eyebrows in answer, winked at Alex, and then took Lucy's hand.

"Bye, Alex!" Lucy waved. Alex blew her a kiss.

Henrietta grabbed the box of tissues and handed one to Alex. "I'm hoping those are happy tears and not sad ones." She sat on the bed.

"They are undecided tears, Henrietta. I really don't

know what to do."

"If you marry Charles, you marry the mountain. Everyone will be glad to see you become part of the family."

Family. That's what it felt like. Family. And home. They made her feel welcomed from the start, and she wanted to embrace that feeling forever...if she could only make it work. "How many people would resent me because of Sharon?"

Henrietta fussed with the bed sheets before answering. "A lot of us liked Sharon. A lot of us also wondered why Charles never married her. His father certainly pushed for it. Charles needed to continue the family bloodline...you know that scenario. We had all but given up that Charles would marry when you came along." She patted Alexandra's leg. "You were a breath of fresh air when you came onto our mountain. You put love into Charles's heart and hope back into ours. You brought Lucy out of her shell and encouraged James to claim what was rightfully his. All of us felt the love you so cleverly hide. Even Sharon felt it. Unfortunately, it put her over the edge." She paused. A sad mask fell over her face. Her gaze was blank as she stared at the wall behind the bed.

"They found Natalie. Nothing but bones. The trees you landed on had a few years of growing, so God put you right into its nest. For Natalie, the trees weren't big enough. She dropped straight down." She shuddered. "I never thought Sharon was capable of such atrocities."

"How's Mr. Billings handling all this?"

"He's furious, of course. He was as blind as the rest of us."

Alex put her head back against the pillow. "He's

paying for my care."

"Yes, he paid for Lucy's when she was here. He put some money toward Sharon's care, but he won't keep that up. I doubt he will ever look her in the face again."

"I'll have to thank him."

Henrietta smiled and patted her leg. "When you feel strong enough, you can march straight up to the manor and announce yourself. Listen, honey." She took Alex's hand. "I'm not here to tell you what to do. That decision must come from your own heart. I'm going to tell you that Charles wasn't the only one who fell in love. You touched every single one of us who met and talked to you. That never happened before from a guest on our mountain. It was like our destiny fulfilled. Even if Charles hadn't fallen in love, we would still try to convince you to stay. All of us felt you belonged on that mountain. I can't explain why." She paused to give Alexandra's hand a light squeeze. "I can tell you that if you want to be a well-renowned doctor, you *won't* be happy on our mountain. If, however, you want to have a family, be a doctor, and have this wonderful man who is absolutely crazy about you, then you *will* be happy on our mountain. Charles will not leave Billings Mountain for any length of time so your decision must be unconditional."

"You put into words what I already felt, Henrietta, that he won't leave for me."

"I'm sorry, Alexandra. His roots are firmly implanted on the mountain. If you decide to leave, the rest of us will be there to help him pull through."

Alexandra looked at her squarely. "You're telling me that his love for the mountain is stronger than his love for me."

"In essence, yes. Don't misunderstand. His love for you is deep. He almost killed Sharon when he found out she threw you off the cliff. I have never seen him display such fury. The men had a difficult time prying his hands off her throat."

Alex envisioned the fury, the uncontrollable rage, both from a man who cared deeply. How could she possibly give that up? She shifted her butt. "I saw something else that night, something I thought I'd never see. He cried." She also saw a man who kept himself separated from the crowd. Why, she wondered, when she sensed such a family unit from the people on the mountain, a community in which he purposely stood to the side. Or above them. Yes, that was the word. Above them. The one in charge. He hid his tears from the others because he had to.

Dumbest conclusion ever.

"He's a proud man," Alex said finally.

Henrietta nodded. "He keeps his feelings bottled up, but even he knew that the Rosebay cliff was a straight drop down from heavy mining eons ago. None of us expected to find you alive. So Charles' emotions went in full circle from intense fury to absolute joy. When he realized it was your blood smeared all over his white shirt, he completely lost it. He loves you very much. Right now, he's working himself silly just to keep his mind occupied. He's constantly checking his cell phone to see if it's working."

Alex smiled at that. "I told him to stay away so I could think."

"And?"

"I couldn't think."

She snickered. "You're in love with him as much as he is with you. I saw it in your eyes that night at the star party."

"Why do you think my decision to stay is so damn hard?"

"It shouldn't be hard at all, dear. You and Charles should be able to work out anything. Love is like that. Just sit down together and have a good discussion about everything that bothers you."

Yeah, money, careers, where to live, where to work. Hard choices, all of them.

"A while back, Charles asked me to keep an open mind. Do you have any idea what that means?"

"Yes, but that's for him to explain. He'll tell you in due time." She slipped off the bed. "It's time I met James and Lucy. We promised Lucy her pizza."

"Maybe you should take Elmo with you. I won't be here much longer."

"Good idea." She took the doll.

"Henrietta, who's Caroline?"

Henrietta's brown eyes twinkled. "A nurse who took care of Lucy. I'm hoping James can rekindle the flame. He deserves a good woman, too." Her face brightened as a light bulb flashed. "I just had a fantastic idea. You can be our doctor, and Caroline can be your nurse!"

Alex laughed. "You're a calculating devil. The next thing I'll hear is you're giving me a corner of the store for my office."

"Ooohhh!" Her eyes widened playfully. "That's not a bad idea at all!" She kissed Alex on the forehead then collected her purse.

"Would you give Charles a message for me?"

"Of course."

"Tell him my chest tube is due to come out. Ask him if he wouldn't mind stopping by tomorrow."

"I'll tell him. Anything else?"

Alexandra smiled at her. "Tell him I missed him terribly."

Chapter Twenty-Seven

Something tickled her hand. She shook it away, so used to the spiders crawling around in her apartment. But she wasn't in her apartment. Alexandra opened a pair of sleepy eyes to see a table lamp lit and the curtains drawn. The sun had set. How long ago, she had no idea.

Something again tickled her hand. She rotated her head to see Charles sitting by the bed. He wasted no time when their eyes met. He stood up, leaned over, and kissed her. Only his lips touched, warm, tender lips that kissed with an intensity that went straight to her soul. His hands clutched the bedrails on opposite sides of her head. His huge body hovered, casting her in a shadow. He looked enormous.

His lips moved away. She reached up and pulled him right back. She wanted so much for him to hold her, but she was still that fragile piece of glass.

"Gad, I missed you," he said softly. His warm gaze scanned every inch of her face. "I couldn't wait until tomorrow. As soon as Henrietta relayed your message, I flew over here. How's the chest feel?"

"Great without the tube sticking in my side. They might release me tomorrow if my X-rays are good."

"Dr. Tagleone told me when I got here. I almost kissed her." He sat again.

"My big problem, is released to where?"

"My place, of course. You will have trouble taking care of yourself with one arm—no protests, please. I insist. I won't put you back in Rosebay alone."

She could see the idea excited him, but there was much to discuss. "Can we talk?"

He took her hand and kissed it. "Talk."

She really didn't know where to begin. Not like she rehearsed the words in her head. "You know how much I enjoy being a doctor," she began.

"It shows."

"You must also know it will be impossible for me to give it up."

"You don't have to. Billings Mountain desperately needs a doctor. I'm going to make an office for you in my house."

Lucy was right after all. She bit her lip.

"Go on, Alex."

She met his questioning gaze. "Charles, there is no way I can hang out a shingle without malpractice insurance. The law is very specific about that. A lot of hospitals pay the insurance for their staff physicians. A lot of private practices pay the insurance also. I can't afford to pay it on my own. I still have my huge student loan, and my bank account is nothing more than an account number. Granted, Virginia's rates should be substantially lower than New York's so I'm guessing $40,000 a year, in that area. I can't afford it."

His eyes grew in size. He sat back in his chair, stunned. "Are you shittin' me?"

"No. So now you see my problem. I want to continue being a doctor, but I can't be a doctor on Billings Mountain. The client base is too small to help pay for that insurance. I'll need to supplement my income by operating in Roanoke or in a private practice somewhere in the valley. The high cost of malpractice insurance is probably why Billings Mountain can't attract a doctor."

He stared. "I'll be damned."

"I have a proposition for you."

"I'm listening."

"You can come to New York with me—"

"Absolutely not. Next option."

"You didn't let me finish."

"I will not leave Billings Mountain for any reason. It's my home."

"Then I will return—"

"No!"

"Charles, you've got to let me finish a sentence! I can accumulate some money—"

"I want you here with me."

"It will only be—"

"No!"

The man was downright frustrating. She let out a heavy sigh. "If you're going to be this obstinate, we may as well stop this discussion right now."

His mouth opened then shut. A grin curled one corner of his mouth while he took her hand and kissed it. "You are going to be a handful, Alexandra. Let's continue our discussion, and I will let you finish your sentences."

"Gee—thanks." She put her head back on her pillow and closed her eyes. "I thought I was strong enough for this. I guess not. I'm tired."

"Then let me talk for a while." He stood to his feet and wandered haphazardly about the room. He walked with his hands in his pockets, chin down, face deep in thought. For some reason, everything about him seemed an exaggeration of seriousness. There was even a hint of amusement on his face.

She definitely needed to get her eyes checked.

"What you're telling me," he began, "is that we won't have enough money to pay for your student loan and malpractice insurance."

"And license."

He stopped in his tracks. "A license, too? You're getting expensive, Alexandra."

"Being a doctor is a business today. We have license and insurance requirements plus we must keep up required credits to hold onto that license which also costs money. I'd love to simply take care of people without worrying about anything else, but we have to eat."

They stared at each other for some time in total silence. She expected this reaction from him. She could see his mind working to come up with a solution. There wasn't a solution. Neither of them had the money to make it happen.

"It won't work, Charles. You won't leave Billings Mountain, and I can't afford to practice there. Even Dr. Tagleone's offer won't solve our problem."

He cocked his head. "What offer?"

"She wants me to consider heading her surgical residency program."

"Here in Roanoke?"

"Yes."

"A hundred and fifty miles away?"

"It's closer than New York."

He stood at the foot of the bed, his gaze intense, his jaw tight. "I have some money saved. We could—"

"No, I will not let you deplete your bank account."

"You're interrupting my sentences now. What I have is yours, you know."

"Thank you, but I won't take it. I have an expensive profession. I'll figure something out."

He frowned, deep in thought. "It's time to get H.C. Billings involved."

"Oh, dear Lord, Charles! The man is already paying this hospital bill. If we ask him to help me set up a clinic, the poor man will never get a return on his money. The client base isn't there. No, I won't ask him."

"Why not? The guy's loaded. I'll call him." He took out his phone.

"Don't you dare!"

"He always wanted a doctor on the mountain. This is his chance. He'll have a personal physician." He punched in numbers.

"Hang it up, Charles. I won't ask him."

"But I will. He can afford to pay your bills, Alex."

She shook her head in disagreement. "I've never known anyone with money who just gave it away. He will have some strings attached. I'll probably have to give him my first born."

Charles gave her a warm smile. His whole face lit up with it. She checked herself just to make sure her hospital gown still covered her vital parts.

"Billings is a nice guy, Alex. Maybe you can arrange a business venture of some sort. Think about a proposal."

Alex groaned.

"I don't want to lose you because of money problems. He's worth a shot." He put his phone away.

"You won't need to approach him right away. I'll take you home with me tomorrow, and we'll talk more about it." He leaned over for a kiss. "I want you with me forever, woman. Sharon almost destroyed the greatest love of my life. I won't let money get in the way. We'll work it out." He touched her chin. "I'm staying at a hotel a few blocks from here. I doubt they'll discharge you early."

"No, X-rays first."

"All right then, I'll see you in the morning." He leaned over for another kiss, a deeper more stimulating kiss. The man still melted all her bones. "Tomorrow," he whispered.

With a light step, he left the room.

Chapter Twenty-Eight

As a doctor, Alexandra never understood why her patients begged and pleaded to be released from the hospital. Bribes galore poured out of their mouths as they relentlessly fought to find that one special weakness to break her. Of course, they never could. And with good reason. Alexandra Colter never stayed in a hospital as a patient. She never experienced the bored-out-of-her-skull dilemma; the constant flipping of TV channels hoping something would grab her attention and occupy the brain for a few hours. Now, she understood. An intense feeling of freedom hit as Nadine wheeled her out of the room. It intensified in the elevator, through the lobby, through the main doors. Air rushed through her hair. Sunlight warmed her face. Freedom.

She would ask for chocolate chip cookies for all the bribes.

"Your man should be along any second now," Nadine said.

They waited by the tarmac where several other wheelchairs sat in a line looking like a train waiting.

"If you don't mind me getting a little personal, Doc, your man is one handsome hunk. I could bite into him any day."

"I think it's going to be nibble-nibble for a while."

A chuckle rose from deep within Nadine's throat.

"You two are so much in love. I can't imagine what a sponge bath would be like."

Alex jerked in the wheelchair. The thought never entered her mind!

Nadine burst out laughing. "Honey, you should see your face! I'll bet he's looking forward to it."

Alexandra bit her lip on that piece of news. He may look forward to it, but she would die of embarrassment. *Oh, God*! *What should I do*?

Charles pulled up in a brand new SUV. Red, of course. He lifted her bodily from the wheelchair to the SUV as if she just had bilateral hip surgery. They said their goodbyes to Nadine, but when he turned to buckle her in, their eyes locked. He kissed her. She kissed him right back. So much love flowed through his lips. She wanted to feel it forever. "You're mine," she whispered.

"Without question." His face glowed. "We'll work things out."

She knew in her heart they would...somehow.

When Charles eased the SUV into traffic, she made the inevitable statement. "I can't believe you bought a new vehicle!"

"It's yours."

Her mouth dropped. "Mine?"

"Sharon destroyed your tin can. You'll need a vehicle."

"You bought this?"

"Yes, it's from me. Do you like it?"

"It's too expensive!"

"That's not what I asked you."

"All right, yes, I love it." Her hand brushed the upholstery. "It's very comfortable."

"That's the main reason I bought it. I couldn't see you in the Red Baron for our trip home. Besides, you'll need a four wheel drive in the winter if you're out playing doctor."

"Our trip home," he'd said. Billings Mountain. Home. Family. An overwhelming sense of happiness filled her.

"That's Billings Mountain straight ahead," he said proudly.

Yep, a mountain straight ahead. He could claim it was Mount Everest. Same thing. No clue. "Charles, about my staying with you—"

He glanced at her. "Yes?"

"I don't feel comfortable with you being my total caregiver."

"Why, you don't think I can do it?"

"No."

He grinned. "You're right. I made arrangements. My housekeeper will be there for your everyday needs. To help her, Mrs. O'Reilly jumped at the chance. Between those two, you can work out some sort of schedule." He gave her a quick sideward glance. A sly smile came with it. "There is no way in hell I can bathe or dress you without severe consequences. Dr. Tagleone said to give your bones a good six weeks to heal. It's going to be a long six weeks, I'll tell you."

She smiled at that because she very much agreed with him.

"Dr. Tagleone also gave me the name of a doctor in the valley," he continued. "He'll be your follow-up physician so we won't have to drive back and forth to Roanoke. Have you thought of what you'll say to Billings?"

"No. All I think about is you."

"Really?" His grin broadened. "You'll have plenty of time to think of a presentation. He's not a hard man to please. Now that you're more than a guest, it's time you met him."

"Yeah, Mr. Enigma. Maybe he will give me a tour of the house."

"Oh, he will for sure. In the meantime, sit back and enjoy the ride."

An excellent suggestion.

Charles pointed out sights as they sped along. He talked of local history and kept up a light one-sided conversation. Unfortunately, the hum of the tires along with super comfortable seats lulled her into a dream-like state. His voice faded. She watched him as he talked, her head resting on the headrest. She heard no words. She saw only his lips move. Nice lips, full, kissable. She drifted off to sleep.

****

Charles woke her with a kiss, a passionate kiss, one meant for bedroom lovemaking. When his lips pulled away, she opened her eyes to see he stood on her side of the vehicle, door ajar. He kept his face barely an inch from her own.

"I love you very much, Alexandra Colter. Do you remember the day I asked you to keep an open mind?"

"Yes. I didn't understand why."

"Then let me explain." He unlatched her seatbelt. She jerked as she looked out the windows. The SUV sat in the circular driveway of the Billings house!

"Oh, God, Charles, not today! I can't think straight let alone try to convince the guy to help finance a clinic. Can't we just go to your place?"

He put his face close. "You are at my place," he whispered.

She looked at that wide staircase leading up to the porch, half expecting to see his name on a mailbox somewhere. "You live here with Billings?"

He chuckled. "You are as naïve as you are beautiful," he said with a smile. "Do you want to put that diagnostic brain of yours to work? Think about it, sweetheart. How much do you know about me?"

Not very much at all, she thought. Then the realization of one fact hit like a brick. She stared, wide-eyed and amazed. "I don't know your last name!"

"No, you don't. You never asked, and I never volunteered."

Her mouth dropped. "You're Billings?"

"Yes, I am Billings. I am Harlan Charles Billings, the owner of this mountain."

Alex went mute.

"While I always wanted a doctor available for the residents, I never expected to fall for one. And I am very much in love with you, Dr. Alexandra Colter. I want to carry you across the threshold as is customary for the Billings men, but I must do it without hurting you. I absolutely do not want to hurt the woman I'm going to marry. Agreed?"

She nodded stupidly, her eyes glued to his face.

"I want children. Do you?"

Again, a stupid nod.

"Say something, Alex."

"The whole mountain was in on this secret?"

"Yes. My ex-wife married me for my money. The divorce cost me a small fortune. I swore it would never happen again. So I became the caretaker, a run-of-the-mill kind of guy with no prospects for the future. Everyone on the mountain had strict orders to call me Charles. When you came along, I gave this charade some serious thought."

"I fell in love with you anyway."

"Yes, you did, and it put me on cloud nine. Sharon never realized that I had no love for the three women she killed. She essentially killed them for nothing, but you, my love, were real from the beginning. Still, you are going to cost me dearly. We will pay off your loan, set up a practice, and if you want to take Eileen Tagleone up on her offer, I can arrange a helicopter to take you back and forth. The choice is yours." He waited for a response. "Say something, Alex."

Tears welled up in her eyes. "I really don't know what to say." She was overwhelmed. With joy. With awe. With astonishment.

"Say you will marry me. Say you will stay in this house, have my children, and be the mistress of this mountain. Say you will grow old with me and be mine forever. Say it, Alex."

The tears streamed down her cheeks. "Why didn't you tell me we weren't going to have money problems?"

He wiped her tears. "It would have given away my entire charade. I will tell you now that we will not have money problems."

"I tormented myself over what to do with my career, damn you. I already knew I wanted you in my life. *And I'm going to live in this house*!"

His face grew serious. "Any questions or doubts, say it now."

The tears flowed. She couldn't stop them if she

tried. She looked into his coal black eyes with affection. "I have only one thing to say, Harlan Charles Billings." She put her hand on his cheek. "It's going to be a long, torturous six weeks!"

To her surprise, he reached over to honk the horn. A crowd flowed through the front door and gathered on the porch, faces she knew, faces she didn't know. Henrietta, James, Lucy, Mrs. O'Reilly, Harry, smiles bright, all clapping. When Charles lifted her in his arms and started up the wide staircase, she peered at them.

"Sneaky little devils! Every last one of you!"

To which they all cheered.

A word about the author...

Jane is a retired respiratory therapist who is married to a wonderful organic farmer. She is an amateur astronomer, an amateur ham radio operator, and an avid people-watcher. She loves to hear or read how two people meet, young and old. When she isn't traveling, she lives in southern New Jersey.

Email: janedrager@yahoo.com
Website: www.janedrager.com